Conrad Richter has written

The Sea of Grass (1937)

Tacey Cromwell (1942)

The Free Man (1943)

The Trees (1940) *which is continued in*

The Fields (1946) *and*

The Town (1950)

Always Young and Fair (1947)

The Light in the Forest (1953)

The Mountain on the Desert (1955)

The Lady (1957)

The Waters of Kronos (1960)

and a volume of short stories

Early Americana (1936)

These are Borzoi Books,
published in New York by Alfred A. Knopf

THE WATERS
OF KRONOS

The Waters of Kronos

BY *Conrad Richter*

Alfred A. Knopf · New York

1 9 6 0

L. C. CATALOG CARD NUMBER: 60–7297

© Conrad Richter, 1960

This is a BORZOI BOOK, published by ALFRED A. KNOPF, INC.

37048

FIRST EDITION

For

Joe and Fred

CONTENTS

THE WATERS
OF KRONOS

The River

For seven days the man who lived by the Western Sea had driven eastward toward the place where he was born, and every day he asked himself the same question. Why had he come? Of course he knew that he had not been well. No one was more aware than he of the lightheaded spells that came over him at times. But why, he wondered, did he suppose he would be better at his destination? It was true that the sailor came home from the sea, the hunter from the hill and the prodigal son to his father's house. But for him there was no longer any father's house to come to. And still he went on, even now when, less than twenty miles from his native valley, fresh misgivings seized him.

It was the first voices of home that particularly disturbed him, those peculiarly flat sounds of speech of his childhood that brought to light long-forgotten memories and feelings.

He passed fields which still slanted as in his boyhood. On the far hills hung the soft blue remembered mists of abundance and fertility. The country had hardly changed. The grazing cattle inclined as always their heads to the earth while the church steeples of his people still pointed to heaven.

The road turned and Shade Mountain stood framed in the windshield. As a boy he had felt mixed emotions for that long forested wall shutting him and Unionville from the world. He had thought it high, wild and almost impassable then. Later, after the lofty ranges of the West, it had seemed little more than a hill. But, curiously, it stood high and wild again to-day.

Three ways there were to cross Shade Mountain, two steep yellow roads torn from the rocks and rock oaks of the sides, and a third through Kronos Gap. The latter was opening magically ahead of him now, revealing the backs of plenty more mountains beyond, the Second, Sharp, Red, Broad, Jeffs and Cantrell, a whole herd of them that had yielded wild milk to his youth. In the center, like the well of a cup surrounded by its circling walls, lay the place he was seeking. His Grandfather Morgan had called it the Vale of Union in his sermons. His Great-Grandfather Scarlett had helped to

name the town Unionville before going to fight the War of
1812. And his Great Aunt Teresa had celebrated both
names in numerous poems that had been printed in the
Unionville Herald and the *Lutheran Messenger,* which her
brothers edited in Philadelphia.

A few lines from one of those poems came to him now, lines
the great-nephews and -nieces used to bandy around as a
family joke.

"Well, how's everything?" they would write, "in:

> *Blest village and vale*
> *Whose mountains fence*
> *In thy eternal innocence.*"

But the man didn't smile today. He had entered the
shadow of the Gap and saw Kronos, the mysterious dark
river, running beside the road, old as the earth it came from,
rising in the spring sands of a score of mountains, trickling
down ravines and hollows, watering ferns and mosses, swell-
ing in hundreds of runs. It came from abandoned mine holes,
too, from old workings deep and silent in the earth to make
at last the river that ran under Unionville's three bridges.
Why, that stream was more familiar to him than the sky! As

a boy he had known it clear enough for swimming although it left the rocks bright orange with sulphur. Later it was black with coal dirt. Still later most of the mines had shut down and the state had cleared up the rest with sumps and laws. The water was clear enough now, they said. They hardly had to treat it for the turbines. It was only the coal dirt still on the river bottom that made it look dark. And yet the sight of it today, the very name that rose to the man's lips, troubled him.

He felt relieved when beyond the Gap the road left the dark stream to pursue its own fancy over the hills and hollows, "hivvily up and hivvily down," as they used to say around home, mimicking the farmers, a road with thick hemlocks in the ravines, wheat and clover on the sunny hill-tops, a white concrete road gray with age, black with the patchings of years and streaked with brown where dirt roads entered and took off.

See, he reassured himself. It's like always. It would be all right. He could take it. He found the frame houses of Crouse's Corners almost unchanged. Beyond, a new and higher road had taken to the hills. Suddenly the road came out on a bluff and he saw at last what he had dreaded, the high concrete dam breast like the white end of a colossal burial vault whose lid was blue water running back for miles, shutting in forever his grandfather's Vale of Union, reaching high on the hills and clasping every hollow.

He stopped the car, a little shaken. He reminded himself that he had known all this. It was no surprise. He had warned himself he must expect modern progress, must realize that the turbines down in their concrete power house together with the giant lines that rose in huge steps over the mountains benefited humanity. Of all people he should be able to look at it in a large way.

And yet he couldn't shake off the feeling that under his feet he had come upon something frightening. He had had a glimpse, small as it was, into an abyss whose unfathomable depths were shrouded in mist, a bottomless chasm that he had known existed, if only in the back of his mind and in the back of everyone else's mind, but which he had never seen face to face or directly looked down into before. Perhaps one had to be old as he to recognize what one saw, to understand first how man had struggled up so painfully and so long, and then with that sad knowledge to come upon one's own once living, breathing and thinking people swallowed up in the abyss, given back to primordial and diluvian chaos.

That must be what affected him, he told himself. He thought of all he had once known and loved buried at the sunless bottom of the dark water—the red roofs and green trees, the life and talk and tender thought that went on under them; the brave brick schoolhouse and its white belfry; the shining railroad and its yellow and brown station; his grandfather's church that skilled hands had put together of stone; the mill that ground the town's staff of life and the shirt factory that had covered the men's backs; the old blacksmith shop which, the last time he saw it, served as an automobile body shop; the gas service station where the old tannery had stood; and his father's frame house where his mother long ago with her bare white hands had thrown a blazing oil lamp out of the window.

The man started the engine of the car and presently turned down the grand new concrete road toward the dam. What was that about facing your worst enemy? Well, here he was. But a high woven steel fence stopped him.

"I'd like permission to go in," he told the man who came to the door of the gatehouse.

"What for?" the guard wanted to know.

"I'd like to go down the Unionville road."

"You can't do that. There is no such place any more. It's down under the lake."

"I know that," the man explained patiently. "I thought perhaps I could stand on the breast a little and look around."

"Nobody's allowed on the breast. Or the shore line two miles either direction. Some radicals once threatened to blow it up."

"I don't want to blow up anything," the man said mildly. "I was just born down here."

"So were a lot of other people, and some of them come most every day and try to get in. They say what you say. They want to go back to Unionville. They want to see if they can tell nearabouts where their houses stood. Or somebody else's house or store. Some of them even want us to take them out in a boat so they can see better. They act like they expect to find a roof or church steeple sticking out of the water. One woman wanted us to drain the lake so she could get some money from her father's cellar where she had a notion it was buried. Oh, you'd be surprised at people if you ever had this job. Most of them that come here would drive you nuts, especially those from this batty place, Unionville."

The man passed a hand across his eyes.

"I don't think it was more batty than any other place," he said quietly.

"Well, you'd say so if you'd been on this job like me. You'd think we were some enemy coming in here instead of our own government. You'd think we were making a ruin and shambles out of their valley instead of a wonderful lake to stop floods and light up half the Eastern Seaboard. Why, some of them tried every trick they knew not to give up their property. They thought they could beat the law. One said he never would get out. He said his people had farmed his farm for four generations. But he got out just the same. I remember one old woman came over to the gatehouse and gave me a spiel before she left. She said her double-great-grandfather fought in the French and Indian War and her great-grandfather in the Revolution and her father in the Civil War. I listened to her till I got fed up. Then I said, 'Well, maybe now you know how the Indians felt when you run them off their land.' "

The visitor gazed back at the guard sadly.

"I don't think that poor woman ever run anybody off her land. My people lived here for four generations."

"Well, it don't do any of you much good now," the guard said.

The man sat awhile in his car.

"I believe there's still a cemetery or two above water. I think I have the right to visit the graves of my people."

The guard looked stony.

"There's a bunch of them. Which one do you want?"

"The Lutheran in town. The New Lutheran. I think it was called St. John's."

The guard came back with a file of dirty-looking papers.

"What's the name?"

"Well, the Donners are buried there and the Morgans and the Scarletts."

"I mean your name."

"John Donner," the man said.

The guard looked up.

"Haven't I heard about you? Aren't you the fellow wrote a book about this town?"

"I probably did. I've written a good many."

"Well, they made this one in a moving picture. I remember hearing you had some kin buried here. I'll make out a pass for you."

He wrote on a slip of paper fastened by perforated edges into a book. But he didn't tear it off. He would rather talk now.

"You're a man who went to school, Mr. Donner. Don't you think bringing those cemeteries up here about the most foolish thing the government ever did?"

"I don't know," the man said. "At any rate it was holding back against the darkness."

"Holding back? It was giving in, if I know anything. They'd never have done it except for the newspapers making such a fuss about turning water on the graves. They said nobody could ever come back and visit them. Now I ask you, what difference does it make once you're dead whether you're covered up with ground or water or both? A lot of our boys were lost at sea but they didn't try to bring them back, did they? Well, they had just about as tough a time here. In some of the old graves they couldn't find much of anything. But they went ahead just the same. They even had drawings made beforehand. Then they dug up the whole shebang and put it back together up here on the big hill. It cost a fortune, but are the people satisfied? Every grave that was down there is up here, but still the people kick and say it isn't like being at the real cemeteries down there."

"There are some things the government shouldn't try to do," the man said.

"What do you mean?" the guard came back. "I thought the government could do anything."

"I wish it could," the visitor said. He wouldn't say more. The guard tried to engage him again without success. He tore off and handed out the slip of paper.

"Well, this'll take you in. You go down here about a quarter-mile and turn to your left. You'll see the sign. I'll phone the guard down there and tell him who you are. He'll show you around.

"I'd rather if he just let me in and let me go around by myself," John Donner said.

"Well, if you say so. I'll tell him that. I'll phone Mr. Otis, too, and see if I can get you a pass to the dam. I'll tell him who you are. I'll say you like to be alone. He might open the place to somebody like you."

"Thank you," John Donner said and drove slowly down the fine new cement road.

CHAPTER TWO

𝕾𝖎𝖑𝖙

A turn in the road hid the lake. For a moment it seemed that he was really going home, back to the old town and its familiar scenes. Then the heavy blot of water reappeared and he found a secondary road leading off to the left, marked CEMETERIES. This he followed until ahead he saw what looked like flocks of sheep grazing on the hillside, but all the time he knew that the white dots were too evenly spaced for sheep.

The first sign read ST. PETER'S LUTHERAN CHURCH. PARKING. That, he remembered, was what they called the Old Lutheran in Unionville, the church from which the New Lutherans had sprung, and he drove slowly on to the next sign. JACOB'S LUTHERAN was what everybody called the White Church in the country below town. He remembered that his Grandfather Morgan's horse, Mike, would of himself on a Sunday turn off the road into the White Church

grounds and shed which on weekdays he passed without
notice. Aunt Jess said that Mike, being a horse, had no
hopes of getting to heaven, but he knew a good deal more
than many Christians who had.

The third sign, CHURCH OF THE BRETHREN, puzzled him.
It must be the Dunkard Church from the Big Dam built
back in the eighteen twenties to feed the canal. During the
Civil War it had broken and flooded the town, drowning
many, an omen and symbol of the future that few had paid
attention to then. John Donner had never seen the Big Dam
in water, but he had seen the Dam Church, as his Grandfather Morgan wryly called it sometimes, and once his
mother's maid, Annie, who always wore her Dunkard cap
even under the sunbonnet, had taken him as a small boy
along to the Dunkard Love Feast. He remembered that he
wasn't allowed to sit with Annie and the other women but
had to go alone to the men's side, where he had never forgotten the ecstatic pleasure on the violent face of a red-
bearded man when a black-bearded brother ceremoniously
washed his red hairy feet.

Well, that was three cemeteries. The fourth he came to
now, ST. MARK'S REFORMED AND TRINITY LUTHERAN. It
took him time to figure that out. It must be, he decided,

Kinzell's, known for miles for its festivals and feuds. John Donner could see it in his mind now, a grim old weather-beaten country church standing in its grove of dark pines. There had been something stark, almost sinister about this church to him as a child. He had thought Pap-pa very brave to go there and read the law from the bare pulpit. But then Pap-pa was afraid of neither man nor devil, and they said that half the crowds at his funerals came to hear what unpredictable things he would say. Like the time he preached the sermon of a Kinzell church member who had once joined a dubious lodge, which attended the funeral in a body.

"We've lost a pillar of the church," they said Pap-pa preached. "He will be sorely missed. The community can hardly do without him. But if certain of you lodge members had died, it would be a different story. The community could easily do without you. You'd be missed nowhere except at some bar or tavern where your rump has worn its mark into the wood, or at the house of some woman, not your wife, where you have no decent or moral right to enter." Oh, Pap-pa had a strong tongue when he chose to speak his mind. During the Civil War his sermons for the Union irked the Copperheads who claimed the war was fought only over "a few niggers." They threatened to tar and feather him but the most they did was roach the mane and tail of his horse while he was preaching.

John Donner stopped the car at the sign, ST. JOHN's, the last of the group, his grandfather's church, St. John's Lutheran. There certainly had been a lot of Lutherans around here, most of them ruled over by Pap-pa. And now the man himself lay among them, his strong tongue silenced, his humorous mind at peace, his tireless form still.

Leaving his coat and hat in the car, the visitor walked over to the cemetery gatehouse. A guard looked up the names he mentioned, made notes on a card, then set briskly off with him in tow. It was like an army cemetery, the visitor noted, spread like a huge fan, the whole mechanically designed and executed, with graves very close together, each headed by a small marker exactly like its neighbor's, all precise and impersonal as the tiers of an outdoor auditorium, which it resembled.

They passed silently through the maze. Each white stone bore its number, name and year of birth and death. Nothing more. The guard consulted his card from time to time and stopped presently at white stones no different from all the rest. John Donner looked down and saw the lettering:

€lijah &. Morgan

1827—1899

738

"This is the first grave you asked for," the guard said briefly. "I'll wait till you're ready and take you to the next."

"If you don't mind," the visitor said, "I'd rather be alone."

"Just as you say. I'm instructed to follow your wishes. You'll note every grave is numbered. I've jotted down the numbers of the people you asked for. Most of them are right around here, but some are elsewhere. If you follow the numbers, you shouldn't have too much trouble." He handed the visitor the penciled card, then marched back the way he had come.

John Donner waited till the sound of footsteps had died out on the grass. He looked back to the stone.

So this was where Pap-pa was finally put to rest, with no more of a marker than anyone else, he who had baptized eleven thousand souls, worn out twelve horses, ruled three congregations and two wives. The second wife lying beside him, Palmyra H. Morgan, No. 739, had outlived him but she had not been mother to his children or grandmother to John Donner. His real Grandmother Morgan he had never seen. Where was she now? Mary Scarlett Morgan, 1828–1867, almost lost in the shuffle, five or six graves away from her spouse, and yet she had borne all his children, dying at thirty-nine from a fall at a picnic. Her daguerreotype showed the strongest face of the family with deep-set eyes like a female Cromwell. Her grandson recalled that this was the second time her body had been moved, the first only a year or two after interment, when the monument was erected. The grave diggers had come to Pap-pa in excitement. Four men could hardly lift the coffin, they said. They were sure the body had turned to stone. They wanted permission to open the coffin. But Pap-pa had been adamant and refused.

About him now, nearer than his first wife, lay her sisters and brothers-in-law, clergymen like himself. Here were two who had never married, Rosemary Scarlett, who, his mother told him, could recite Shakespeare by the page. She had entertained for her father when he was in the legislature at Harrisburg, and died of consumption at eighteen. Her sister, Teresa, the poetess, lived to be eighty-four, a teacher who took her school on a daily walk and more than once held up a hissing gander helpless by the neck till her charges were past. Her tomb down in the old Unionville cemetery had read "A lover of children." The Scarletts were known for their epitaphs. The Rev. Timothy Scarlett, D.D., L.L.D., had on his late stone "He spoke and taught as one having authority, fervent in the spirit of the Lord," while the stone of his brother, the Rev. Howard Scarlett, D.D., Ph.D., read "A scribe instructed unto the kingdom of heaven, he brought forth out of his treasury things old and new." Their wives, who outlived them, had no epitaphs.

Now where was his Great-Grandfather Scarlett, a captain in the War of 1812, squire, legislator and "oil inspector under Governor Hiester," or so Aunt Teresa used to say? Down in the Unionville cemetery his name graced a marble monument, a shaft of twenty feet as befitted his station. Here he was just No. 732, reduced almost to oblivion, his silent wife beside him. John Donner couldn't remember ever seeing a picture of him. Beyond lay his own favorite Aunt Jess with Uncle Dick Ryon, who had once lived in Colorado and Florida, very briefly as befitted an Irishman who couldn't resist telling his employers off. Their daughter, Polly, who had been one of the closest of cousins to the Donner boys, was nearby, but her two husbands had been buried elsewhere as had her son, the idol of the "freind-schaft," dead of diphtheria at eight years.

All the while the visitor held in his mind the two graves that mattered most. In the Unionville cemetery he had gone to them straight off before any other, seeing nothing else for a time than the pair of strong upright granite slabs with the deeply carved letters, the Rev. Harry A. Donner and Valeria M. Donner. It had consoled him to find them in such a favored place, on the big Morgan-Scarlett lot, one of the pleasantest spots on the hill, where the ground began to slope gently toward the south. The sun lay warm on the graves in winter so that the snow always melted here first and there was a superb view of the valley and mountains. But today he had trouble coming on their names and then found them lost in the second row among strangers. He stood for a while staring at them, frowning.

What had he come back here for anyway, he demanded of himself. Was he secretly trying to find a final resting place for himself? When young, he would have rejected the thought instantly. Now he wasn't so sure. It was true that fire had never appealed to him. He had thought scattering your ashes rather a conceited thing, making a rite out of the trifling and profane, as if the landscape you loved cared.

Also, he wasn't certain that it wasn't a form of escape, to avoid the prospect of long decay, a kind of claustrophobia about being put underground. He himself had thought to follow the courage and custom of his ancestors. But where, he had never decided. The depositories of his Western city had seemed too cold and impersonal. Their sleepers didn't know the names of the sleepers next to them. One winter in Georgia he had considered the South. The cheerfulness of the darkies who served him and of the woodsmoke that came from their cabins appealed to him. But he would still be alien there, and a perpetual dampness seemed to mildew the ground. The New Mexico country he loved would be drier. Some of his best friends lay in that desert land, moldering painlessly away into dust to be blown someday over the country. Nowhere did graves look more lonely and abandoned. He remembered what an old rancher sixty miles from a railroad had once said to him.

"Next year I may be in the ground. But I hope you'll come just the same. It'll be mighty lonesome a-layin' way out here where no human hardly passes."

Was that why he had come back to where the air was peopled with the multitudinous imaginary forms of his youth? The rancher had told him that horses raised and

broken around ranch headquarters nearly always returned
from the open range to die. He didn't know why but he
thought they wanted to be near man again. It was as if the
horses had remembered man as a god, and when old age came
over them they looked back in their dim horses' minds to
when they had been young and strong in companionship
with that god and came back in the hope that their god
could help them. Was that, John Donner wondered, the
unreasoning impulse deep in his own mind, driving him
back to this place?

He turned away. Whatever he had sought, it was not
here. The place was spurious. The old cemetery at Unionville had been genuine, a part of life. Any day and almost
any part of the day, especially toward evening, you could
see the living among the dead, someone bending over a grave
with love and remembrance, running a lawn mower on the
lot, perhaps going with a vase for fresh water or resting on
one of the green benches scattered under the trees, con-
templating life and death or the peaceful scene.

And on Decoration Day the whole cemetery would burst
into spring, a religious symbol, with even the unclaimed lots
trimmed, the hill a flower garden, annual visitors from out
of town mingling with townsfolk, shaking hands, renewing

acquaintance, talking of the past and present, the dead and
the living. A parade would move up from Kronos Street
with soldiers and Boy Scouts in uniform, children in gay
dresses marching and bands playing. Half the town would
be waiting or stream up after. Eventually there would be
the sharp crack of salute by the honor guard to their departed brethren in arms, and some speaker droning lazily
from the back of Lib Fidler's wagon and, later, Ducky
Harris's truck.

But he found none of that up here. With a sense of fu-
tility and defeat he started back to the car. Before reaching
it he came on a small lane, hardly more than wheel tracks
running through an unclosed gate to the north and thence
through an open field. It was a relief to follow it, to get
away where things were natural and real. He went on half
expecting to be called back by the guard but nothing
happened.

Halfway across the field he saw a little old car coming
out of the hollow. It stopped when it came abreast. John
Donner had a glimpse of axes and a crosscut saw in the
back. On the front seat two old men turned faces toward him.

"You can't get anyplace down there, mister. This road
dead-ends."

"Doesn't the Long Stretch road run in that hollow?" Donner asked.

"Well, it does and it doesn't. It's there where it ain't bulldozed away. But it's closed up above by the big steel fence and down below by the water. You can't get up and you can't get down." The old eyes scrutinized him sharply. "You from around here?"

"Once upon a time. My father was Harry Donner. Maybe you knew him."

"Harry Donner! Used to have a store in Unionville before he was a preacher? His father-in-law baptized me. Come to think of it, you mind me of him. Your father, I mean."

"I look like my father?" John Donner asked.

"Well, you do. I ought to know. I buried him. Me and Yuny here. We dug his grave on a cold January morning. Had to build a fire to thaw out the ground."

The other old man, whose pipe reeked of black tobacco, took it out of his mouth.

"What do you think of it up here?" He pointed it toward the cemetery.

"It's not like the one in Unionville."

"It's dead," Yuny said. "Nobody gets buried in it. Nobody digs a grave from one year to another. It's dead as a doornail."

"You know what he means?" the first old man said. "We used to work in St. John's graveyard, him and me. We had a bet on which would bury the other fellow. Now they got to bury us someplace else."

"Something was always going on down in that cemetery," Yuny said. "I could tell you a lot of things. Like the time we had to dig two graves in one day and they got Bob Bender and Ike Zerbe to dig the other one. Bob had his bottle along and when Check here and me went over and seen what they dug, we had to go to the preacher. 'You got to get that straightened out tonight, Parra' we told him. 'There ain't no coffin made'll ever fit that grave.' It was hooked like a sickle. Yep, bent like a quarter-moon. But we got to get home, mister. They lock the gate up here at five thirty."

"Yes, I can see you're a Donner now," the first grave digger said. "You're the picture of your daddy. He done something to me once I never forgot. I was only a boy from Canal Street and nobody wanted me around. They didn't make a fuss over kids those days like they do now. Get out, they'd say to me like I was a cat. Well, on the Fourth of

July I seen your daddy fetch a couple wooden boxes of fireworks and firecrackers from the store. I hung around expecting every minute to get sent home. But your daddy called, 'Come on over here, Check, and set down where you can see and won't get hurt.' You boys was all setting on the curb and he made a place for me alongside. He even let me set off some of the firecrackers. He was the first ever treated me like that, and I ain't forgot it."

When the little old car left, Donner went on the other way. What the old grave digger had said had much moved him. In his mind he could see his father as in the flesh, a strong, hearty man with a black mustache. John Donner had often tasted that mustache as a boy. It had embarrassed him. No other father in Unionville kissed his boys. It wasn't done among the Pennsylvania Dutch. Girls weren't kissed much either. Many a Unionville girl lived all her life without her father showing her affection. Now, her mother might, if the girl had been away from home for a long time or there'd been a death in the family.

But John Donner couldn't say that of his father or mother. He stopped and took a snapshot from his breast-pocket notebook. For years it had stood in a small black frame on his desk at home. Now yellow and soiled, it had started to crack. It was a picture he had taken himself with his father's old plate camera when he was ten. His younger brothers sat at a small table in the old sitting room, their mother between them smiling her warm love at the young photographer. It was a scene that never failed to bring back the old realities, the almost forgotten sideboard with claw feet, the crokinole board standing against the wall, the colored wall-hangings of his mother, the old-time shepherd dog Sandy panting on the floor, and in the background the two closed doors, one to the stairs and one to the kitchen.

Under the door to the stairs he could see nothing, but white light streamed from under the door to the kitchen. Beyond that door, hidden and kept back by it, was something he couldn't name but which in his mind's eye was infinitely bright and rich with the light of youth. Whenever of late years he looked at it, he could feel something inside of him trying to seize the knob of that door and pull it open so he could pass through it into the light. He could feel that intense inner striving now. But nothing happened. He was a fairly able man who had reached honors envied by some other men, but never was he able again to get through that closed door. This, he suspected, was part of the source of the pain that sometimes came to his head, his setting into motion concentration and mental impulses that had always fetched him what he wanted but were brought to nothing now by an old pine kitchen door. Perhaps it was trying to do the impossible that tortured him. He could feel the pain starting in his head again.

He put the snapshot away in his notebook and went on, down over the crest of the hill. The cemetery guard couldn't see him here. Neither could he see lake or cemeteries. They seemed like a dream. This, not that, was the real, he felt, the air blowing from Shade Mountain, the cawing of crows from high up on Summer Hill, the lowering sun lying soft and golden on the unused fields.

The slow peaceful life he had known as a boy remained in this spot. The field was white and sweet with late wild carrot that some call Queen Anne's lace. A groundhog lumbered ahead of him, making for its hole. Deeper in the hollow the serene evening song of robins rose over the quiet scene. A wood thrush called. It must be perched somewhere in the trees that stood along the old road that once led to the mines. They had called it the Long Stretch from the endless grade over the hills and through the mountains to Primrose Colliery.

He came on a vestige of that road presently. Farther down

in the turning hollow he knew it must come to an end in water and above him run futilely into the steel fence. At places, the woodcutters had said, it was bulldozed out. But here for a short distance in the shelter of the hollow it lay untouched and utterly unchanged, the same yellow shale where butterfly weed grew, the same thick velvety leaves of the moth mullein and the bright patches of goldenrod. It even smelled like it used to, like Union Valley had always smelled. He had lived over much of the country and seen more of the world, but he had found no odor like that of the mixed woods and fields where he had been born, the wild scent of native grasses mingled with that of hardwood leaves, hemlock and pine. Old cherry and ash trees stood along the road. After climbing the fence he was glad to lean against one of them to combat the faintness in his head.

He must have stayed there a long time. The longer he stood in the growing dusk, the less it seemed that he had ever gone away. Nothing here had changed. He could almost believe that he was still a youth and that the beloved town and valley lay intact and untouched below. Why, this had been the most familiar road to him around Unionville! As a boy he had coasted down it in winter. Summers he had gone with

his father, who twice a week delivered a three-horse covered
spring wagon of grocery orders to the mining patches on
Broad Mountain. So often had his father passed this spot, he
thought there must still remain in the road some faint tread
of his wagon's tires and impress of his horses' shoes. Standing here now peering through the dim light, he could almost
feel himself a boy coming down from the mountain, sitting
beside his father on the spring seat, the wooden brake
screeching, the horses "rutching" and ahead of him home and
supper waiting in the evening lamplight.

His nerves tautened. Did he only imagine it or was something moving up there on the Long Stretch? Yes, he could
see it now through the trees and dusk. It was coming toward
him on the road, a wagon with a white top like his father's,
three horses, and a gray like old Bob hitched in the lead. The
strangest feeling ran over him. He must be really ill, he told
himself, for there was no open road above for the wagon to
have come from and no place but water below for it to go.
Besides, there were no wagons like that on the road any more.
Men drove trucks. Even the old woodcutters had a car. Yet
he could plainly hear the rumble of the oaken running gear
and the sharp sound of iron horseshoes striking stones in the

road. An inexplicable fear possessed him. Then as the wagon came abreast he saw that the driver was not his father but an old man, older still than he, with long gray mustaches.

If the driver saw him, he gave no heed, driving on grave and preoccupied, the reins in his hand. In another moment or two he would be past.

"Speak to him. Speak to him before he's gone!" John Donner cried to himself.

CHAPTER THREE

The Chasm

And still he stood rooted with a kind of paralysis as in a dream, watching the wagon go on, carrying with it a mysterious brightness about its canvas top, leaving him behind in the gloom of the hollow.

"Wait!" he cried.

The driver looked back, his eyes sad and deep above drooping mustaches, like a face from another world, but he did not stop. John Donner hurried after the wagon.

"Please. May I speak to you?" he begged.

And still the wagon bumped on, lurching, the driver silent. John Donner had the impression the man was incapable of speech. Then, farther down the steep grade, he drew his reins and halted the horses with the front wheels of his wagon resting in a cross gutter. The visitor ran after. Careful, careful what you say, he urged himself. But speak! The man is waiting!

) 33 (

"Can you tell me where this road goes?" he asked.

"Goes? Why, it goes to the mines," the driver said, becoming suddenly real enough, exploding the myth of dumbness.

"I mean the other way." John Donner pointed into the chasm.

"That way goes to Unionville." The driver spat heavy tobacco juice over the wheel and waited.

"But Unionville——" John Donner said and stopped. He had almost said that Unionville was gone, drowned out, never to be seen by human eye again. Careful, careful, he repeated to himself, then aloud, "You mean you're going down there —to Unionville—tonight?"

"Farther'n that. I got to go over the mountain."

So that was why he had three horses in his team. John Donner remembered that the mountain road was steep. He edged closer.

"May I ride with you?" he asked.

"If you're going to Unionville, you can walk it," the driver said. "It ain't far."

"I'm afraid," John Donner confessed, "I couldn't make it alone."

"Afraid of what? You can't miss it. You could close your eyes and you'd run right into it."

"I'd like to ride with you, if I may," the man in the road requested. "I've not been too well."

"Well, it's that much more for the team to hold back. But I guess I can take you." The driver looked at the stranger as at a difficult person, but he made room on the seat.

As he climbed over the wheel, John Donner glanced back into the wagon box. He saw it filled to the sideboards with the deep product of the earth, the residue of life that had flourished countless years ago. So that was the scent he had noticed standing there, the faint, almost imperceptible, yet unmistakable taint of wet, freshly mined anthracite, a mysterious smell, not quite chemical, yet something as a boy he had often detected in the miners' trains and even from men with blackened faces trotting home from the station, the odor of a buried world, very difficult to describe, native to the mouth of the Primrose slope and the dripping depths below. He recalled that when the colliery closed down, they had been mining from the eighth or ninth level, each level eighty yards apart, which meant that he was riding now with a cargo drawn from beneath the level of the sea.

The driver waited till his passenger settled himself on the wooden seat. Then he released the brake and they started down into the chasm.

At every turn John Donner looked for the road to peter out. He thought they must surely come upon spots scraped by the bulldozer to nothingness, must reach the edge of the water. But the old shale road continued to stretch beneath them and around their heads the soft country dusk sweet with the farming scents of early September. A lantern shone in Blinkley's unpainted barn as they passed. He could smell cows. A field of corn shocked in the old-time fashion came down to the rail fence. A horse and buggy went by close enough to be touched by his outstretched hand. Then they came out of the hollow to a familiar level stretch.

This, he knew, was the Breather, where teams coming up the Long Stretch could get their wind before the next grade. And now the lights of the old town were coming into view directly below them, not the bright glitter of electric bulbs but the mildness of oil wicks sending their steady yellow beams among the trees. As a boy he had often coasted to town from here. This was the steepest descent of the Long Stretch, and the horses let themselves into it gingerly, the wagon tongue rising and the horses' collars thrusting out in protest. John Donner had the feeling he was descending from where he could never return.

They passed the white Shollenberger house high on its

long flight of wooden steps, passed the light and dark brown
house of Mr. Kirtz, who drooled on his beard and the green-
groceries he sold in the basement of the Eagle Hotel, passed
the curious blue house where lived the girl in his school who
would never speak above a whisper in class. Years afterward
he heard that she had married and had twins, and he had
always pictured her in his mind whispering to her children
while other Unionville women shouted and threatened.

The wagon was almost down, crossing the alley which the
Uptown boys took going home from school. Beyond, he could
see Kronos Street lying peaceful, leafy and unchanged, with
snug houses under the trees and the Methodist church and
old tannery on opposite corners. The driver took his team
and wagon across without pausing for traffic. Looking up
and down the old street, the passenger could feel an almost
frightening solitude. There were no headlights as far as he
could see. Sleepy lights slanted from a few houses, from the
post office up the hill and from stores scattered among the
dwellings.

"I'll get off here, if I may," John Donner said. The driver
pulled up his horses but his passenger didn't get off. "Are
you acquainted in Unionville?" he asked.

"A little." The driver took a fresh chew.

"Do you know any of the stores?"

"Well, there's Smith and Reinbold, and Kipps, Donner and Company."

At the latter name, the stranger felt a tightening in his chest.

"Do you know if Harry Donner could still be living?"

"Living! I didn't know he was dead! I seen him a month ago up at Primrose delivering in the Patch."

Emotion and a certain excitement came up in John Donner. Suddenly he remembered.

"My coat. I forgot it. I left it up in the car."

"You come on the railroad?" And when the other didn't reply: "Well, first thing I noticed about you was you had no coat and no hat on. A man don't hardly need a coat this kind of weather, but it's unhealthy to go without your hat. It chills the brain. Now, I don't have an extra hat but I have a coat I don't use much. It was Jake Stroud's. His widow gave it to me when he died. You can have it till you get yours. If you don't mind wearing a dead man's coat. It could turn cold on you overnight this time of year."

"Thank you," the stranger said. "I'll leave it at Donner's store for you to pick up next time you come through." He

climbed down over the wheel and waited for the wagon to
pass. It moved by with extraordinary slowness. The driver
lifted his hand good-by. There was something strange about
him, John Donner told himself, but then there had always
been something strange about "die leit ivver der barrick,"
the over-the-mountain people.

He started up the Methodist church hill. How incredibly
quiet and peaceful it was. Nothing had changed. The sidewalk, moist and slippery as when he was a boy, still shone
faintly in the darkness, reflecting unseen light. You had to
lift your feet to keep from stumbling over the unpredictable
bulges where unseen roots had lifted the bricks in giant mole-
like waves. He passed the house of Mr. Nagle, chief clerk for
the Markles, who owned Primrose Colliery. It had the peculiar dreamlike look of certain houses when he was young, of
importance without and hushed withdrawal from the world
within. Across the street the white horse of Dr. Sypher, who
had brought him into the world, stood hitched to the buggy,
head drooping, perhaps asleep. At the top of the hill was
the old post office, tinier than ever in its square boxlike building that had once been a squire's office. It must be after six
o'clock in the evening but the stamp window was still up,

with Katie Gerber calmly reading someone's paper behind the partition of call and lock boxes. No one was visible on the public side. In an hour it would be jammed with townspeople chatting to each other, waiting for the seven-thirty mail from Lebanon to be "changed," everyone keeping an eye on his or her box not to miss when a letter or paper might be popped in.

As he went on, someone emerged from the shadows and came toward him, a boy touching the trees as he passed, darting away from the stranger, tagging the post-office tree by sidling around it like a squirrel, then into the post office with the letter in his hand and out again almost in the same motion, returning down the street he had come. He left in the man a baffled feeling. That slender face he thought he had seen before, but where? And what was his name? Even the shirt the boy had on, a design of stripes and colors he hadn't seen for years, left the man with the strangest sensations.

He stepped into the post office and waited till the brown eyes of Katie Gerber appeared at the high stamp window, severe at the sight of a stranger.

"Can you tell me who that boy was?" he asked.

The brown eyes scarcely changed.

"I heard somebody but didn't notice," she said. Through

the partition he saw her go to the mail drop, lift out the last letter, look at it and drop it back without saying anything. What she had learned was for her own information.

The man went uncertainly back to the sidewalk and down the shadowy street. How fragrant was the air he had grown up in and never noticed, redolent of bark and leaves as of the forest! That was Unionville, he told himself, the combination of town and woods, life going on in these houses under the trees, eating, sleeping, reading, making meals in the kitchen all beneath the giant limbs. He could hear at this moment the faint sounds of a piano and horn from different houses, each pursuing a different tune, reaching him through the inexhaustible filter of leaves. He made his way past the brick house built by one of the tannery owners, and the frame house where old Josie Rehrer lived. Across the street stood the white house where his mother used to send him for milk, through the gate and around to the back porch, where he had to wait till his kettle was filled from a crock on the cellar floor.

They called it the Markle square. You never said block in Unionville. The big Markle house, with a full third floor where the servants lived, gave it dignity. He was coming to Dan Markles' ornamental iron fence now. The heavy gate led to a rounded portico, shaped like a Christmas cooky. There was another portico on the second floor, a conservatory wing on the first and a wonderful room with deep red leather chairs and walls lined with books enough for a lifetime of reading. The Markle square was a long square, and here in the middle of it, far from the lamppost at either end, all was swathed in muffled darkness but he could smell the rich fragrance of an expensive cigar drifting out from behind those closed yellow blinds.

And now he felt a rising constriction. Ahead on the far side of the street he could make out the general store of Kipps, Donner and Company, known in the family as "Papa's store," with a broad store porch and a dozen steps the width of the building rising from the sidewalk, both store and steps unpainted but tacked with a multitude of tin advertising signs, mostly for tobacco. Faint light filtered from the old-time store windows, crude compared to those of today. Like the post office, the store was still open and would be, he knew, long after Katie Gerber closed the post office.

John Donner stood under a tree looking across the street. He felt sure he could make out a man behind the counter. When he went over to the other side the man had disappeared but he thought he heard a familiar voice singing. He knew then it must be his father. As a boy he had sometimes wished his father tuneless like other fathers. Or if he had to do something, why didn't he whistle like many of the Pennsylvania Dutch? He sang incessantly, rousing Sunday-school hymns when he felt good, sad songs when "down in the mouth." "March on, march on, for Christ counts everything but loss," was one of the stirring kind, together with "Onward, upward till every foe is conquered and Christ is Lord indeed." The fervor, that's what his father liked, so he could let himself go. He used to thunder out "Peal forth the watchword, silence it never." "True hearted, whole hearted," was another, and "Speed Away." It had always seemed incongruous to be with his father driving the slow heavy three-horse team with a load of groceries up the mountain and hear him ring out to the culm banks, "Speed away. Speed away. On your mission of light. To the lands that are lying in darkness and night." This was the gospel version. Once in a great while he would sing the real words, "There's a young heart awaiting thy coming tonight."

Chiefly his father sang when active, running up and down the stairs, when going to answer the doorbell, while working with his hands. He seldom sang sad songs except at home. An audience enlivened him, gave him power. He liked people, was stimulated by them. He made his son wince by speaking to everyone he met on the street, male or female, young or old. Not only here in Unionville but in Lebanon, where people looked after him curiously. Uncle Dick said his brother-in-law had once cordially greeted a painted-up whore they passed on Center Street in Pottsville. He also embarrassed his son in church. He sang so much louder than necessary. Charley Miner once said he had looked for Harry Donner in a crowd of a thousand men roaring out "The Star Spangled Banner" in the Rajah Temple in Reading. He could hear him, he said, but he couldn't see him. That was his father to a T. In church the boy imagined everyone staring at them, thinking it was showing off.

Today outside the store the son recognized the song. Its name he didn't know but he was startled by the words. It was almost as if his father knew he was there.

> *"Lift high the latch, my boy, my boy,*
> *And wait outside no more.*
> *There's love and rest, my boy, my boy,*
> *Within thy father's door."*

Gradually he knew better. He had heard his father sing it too often at home. The meaning in the words then and now was hidden. His father, he felt, had always sung at home in riddles, saying in music what he could never bring himself to reveal in speech. As a boy he had thought these particular words a warning to him to give up his youthful, dissenting ways, his shying from church and people, and enter into his father's hearty way of life and religion.

Now his father came back into view behind the counter. At the sight of his unmistakable black mustache and powerful movements, the old restraint the boy felt for his parent came over him. Why, he had asked himself a thousand times, did this stiffness exist between them? Nobody else appeared to feel that way toward his father. His cousin Pol, some few years his senior, adored him. Her brother, Matt, looked up to him, and Matt was no mollycoddle, a member of the bunch that put wagons and buggies in the canal on Halloween. Only he, Johnny, his oldest son, was uncomfortable with him. As a child he couldn't easily fathom it except that his father was not his real but a foster father and that the constriction must come from his side, which was why the boy resented it so keenly, coming from one who was so open, friendly and companionable with everybody else.

Once away from his father, he thought he had outgrown and forgotten it. And yet each time they met again, the incomprehensible constriction would rise between them. The stronger and heartier his father, the more stubborn and powerful the feeling would take form in the son. Standing here outside his father's store after all these years, he could feel it tonight, gripping him without rhyme or reason, holding him back, a grown man, even today. Sometimes he wondered if, whatever it was, it hadn't been the origin of his interest in books and nature, not born of commendable thirst for knowledge, but from a shying away from his father's world of enthusiastic sociability with people, which had given him as a boy only difficulty and suffering so that he found relief in freedom and solitude in fields, the forest and the printed page, like an unreasoning moth released from the hand and soaring in air it had never taken cognizance of before.

He came to himself with a start. Someone was coming up the store steps behind him. Whoever it was must have seen him standing here, peering through the windows. He turned and saw the lynxlike beard of Mr. Paxman, his blue eyes hard as at someone caught spying.

"You want something?" he asked sharply.

"I'm looking for—" John Donner began and caught himself in time. He had almost said "my father." He tried again more cautiously. "I wanted to see if Mr. Donner was here."

"He's gone!" Mr. Paxman informed him.

"But I thought I saw him through the window."

"He's out of business," Mr. Paxman said. "He's going away to study to be a preacher. He sold me his share in the business. You'll have to talk about business to me."

"I don't want to see him about business," the stranger said. "It's personal."

The bearded man looked disappointed. His interest evaporated.

"Well, in that case you'll find him still here. He was helping me out tonight while I went to supper." He stood back, waiting for the other to enter.

Now that he was actually expected to face his father, John Donner froze. He would have retreated, if he could. What could he say that wouldn't make him out an impostor or a lunatic? He was conscious of Mr. Paxman watching him, questioning his hesitation. He forced himself up the remaining steps to the accustomed stout double door. It still bore the old latch, very low down so a child could reach it, of wrought steel, an arc of metal for the hand and a steel trough above so the thumb could press down and lift the catch inside. This he did. The door opened and he went in.

Nobody was there. The familiar store room, still more of a

dark cave than he remembered, stood empty, the old square and slanted glass showcases cloudy and scratched, with the sediment of sugar in the counter cracks, the shelves loaded with multitudinous objects not to be found on the market today. Tinware hung from the high ceiling, and sugar, cracker and flour barrels stood below. He breathed an air compounded of age and dampness, of molasses and cloth dyes, of spices and coal oil, of rubber boots and leather shoes, of tubs of overripe butter and cheese, of bananas black and spoiling on the bunch, all these and a hundred other scents mingled to form the whole and familiar blend. Bracket oil lamps cast shadows on the wall, imprisoned flies buzzed on strips of flypaper, and the bare floor was deeply grooved and worn by the dragging of heavy containers.

Then the stranger heard someone coming up from the cellar, the swift steps he had heard a thousand times, sharp, vigorous, the toe of each shoe striking forward on the steps. The cellar door opened and he saw his father, lamp in hand.

"Here's an old man to see you, Harry," Mr. Paxman said.

The caller winced. Why, it had been Mr. Paxman and his father who had been old, not he. His father looked no more than thirty-five as he set the lamp in its bracket and wiped his hands on a dirty roller towel. He came forward holding out his hand with that hearty ease he always enjoyed with strangers and which somehow impoverished and cramped his son to see.

"I don't think I caught the name," he said, the same unforgettable smile under his black mustache.

"My name is John," the stranger said hoarsely.

His father's eyes searched his face while still holding his hand.

"Haven't we met before?"

"Yes, many years ago." For a moment the son had the feeling that his father was going to recognize him. Then he saw it was only his parent's inveterate interest in people.

"You come from around here?"

"I do, but my people are dead and gone. They're not even buried here now."

"Then you don't live around here any more?"

"No, sir. I've come a long way, longer than I could tell you."

His father nodded politely. He looked up at the wooden clock ticking on the wall. The son saw it was still lettered SALEM THREAD, in black on the glass.

"Mr. Paxman said you wanted to see me?"

The stranger nodded. He saw his father waiting and knew

what he waited for, but how could he tell him what he had come to see him about when he didn't know himself? What could he say at all that wouldn't lead to difficulties and suspicion? He told himself he should never have approached the store. He saw his father watching him intently. In the end he exchanged a meaning look with Mr. Paxman.

"Well, I have to be going down the line," he said.

Panic seized the stranger. He dare not let him go.

"Is the family well?" he stammered.

"Why, yes. Pretty well, thank you."

"You have two other boys, don't you?"

"Three," his father corrected. "Three boys. My wife hoped the youngest would be a girl."

"They're all right, the boys?"

"Tiptop," his father said. The son remembered it was one of his favorite words.

"And my—I mean, their mother? Is she all right?" Anxiously.

"You know my wife?"

"I knew her once long ago. I don't know if she'd remember me now."

"I didn't catch your name."

"John," the stranger said again.

"And your last name?"

"Donner," he said, mumbling it.

"How?" his father asked sharply. His father had always said "How?" instead of "What?"

"Donner. The same as yours." The stranger felt his Adam's apple strain. "When I was young I thought we might be related."

He expected his father to be taken by that, at least struck by the coincidence and mention that his oldest boy bore the same name. But he passed it off in the way of a strong man holding off those who would impose on him.

"There're lots of Donners in Pennsylvania. No connection that we know of. My father had only one sister in this country and an uncle who went to Texas fifty years ago. We never heard of him again. You say you came pretty far. You didn't come from Texas?"

"No, sir," the stranger said regretfully.

"Well, I guess we aren't connected then." His father spoke definitely, finally, cheerfully, settling any excuse for the call, closing the matter. He turned away.

How often had the son seen him turn like this from those who took too much of his time, who came to the store or the house and hung on him, talking too much or too little, staying on and on. But never before had he seen his father turn away from him. Why, his father had always paid him too much attention, despite his shortcomings, his shyness, his inability to feel comfortable with people, to make small talk.

In his mind's eye he could see his parent now in the yellow lamplight of an unearthly night hour. He was standing in his nightshirt in the middle of the back-bedroom floor, holding up with one hand a sleepy small nightshirt-clad boy, with the other hand a white chamber pot while he made endless noises with his lips. "Psssss," he'd say encouragingly. "Pssssssssss," trying to induce the boy to make his water in this safe receptacle and avoid wetting the bed. How many times must his father have done that, crawling out from warm covers night after night, an impatient man patiently conspiring until what he sought had been accomplished. And now he was turning away from one of those same boys. What had happened to him, to them both, to the unsought relationship he had once fancied fixed and unchangeable between them?

His father came out from behind the counter, putting on his hat and coat.

"Well, good night, George," he said to Mr. Paxman, then a civil good night to the old man.

The latter watched helplessly. He was going away without him, down the street to the house the son knew so well, to the red hanging lamp in the hall and the yellow hand lamp in the kitchen. There was no place in the world he would rather go this early September evening. Strange that he had never wanted to go home at night as a boy, when the door had opened to him as a matter of course, when his mother had waited up till he came, and, if late, one of them would come looking for him. But none would come looking for him this night when he needed that house and the people in it more than he had ever needed them before. No one would wait up for him until he came.

His father was outside now, going down the steps, lighting a cigar as he went. He had already forgotten the old man in the store. It is only the young who forget, the latter was thinking. He remembered how the same parent had never let him escape as a boy, calling him to strangers he didn't give a hoot about. "Johnny, I want you to meet these people. This is my son," he'd say proudly as if introducing an important person, putting on a beaming face and tone almost never used at home. It had irritated the boy. He couldn't understand it. Even after he had grown up and left home, his father's letters seldom failed to add, when mentioning people,

"They asked about you," or "They wanted to be remembered," although the son well knew it had been his father who had spoken to them about him so he would be remembered.

There came back to him now the time his father had visited him in Albuquerque. It was while they lived in the adobe house with the blue patio gate. His first book had just been published. The manager at Fred Harvey's had told him of an enthusiastic reader who had praised the book and bought five or six copies at different times to send to friends. One went to England, another to Germany. The author had felt flattered and pleased. Then suddenly he had thought of his father.

"Dad," he had said sternly at dinner that evening. "Have you been buying my book at the depot?"

He would never forget as long as he lived the guilty hurt look of a small boy that came to his father's face. The son wished he hadn't spoken. He would have given him what books he wanted, had he known, but his father had followed his own counsel, gone in secret to the bookseller, praising the author and spending his own scarce money for copies.

At the memory, a melting and yearning for his father swept over him. He wanted desperately to run after, to walk down the street with him, to put his arm in his, a gesture that would embarrass his father today as it would have the son years ago, to express perhaps a word of affection he couldn't recollect ever speaking or even implying. But it was too late. He stepped out of the store. Far down Kronos Street he heard the distant footsteps of his father retreating into the night.

CHAPTER FOUR

Rust

For a long time the stranger stood on the store porch steps listening to the dying footsteps in his ear. Then they ceased. His father had gone where he could not follow. He should have sought home first, he told himself, while his mother was there alone save for his two brothers. Or were there three? The problem confused him. Never mind. His mother was all that mattered. If he were old as Methuselah with a long white beard, he believed that she would still know him.

Now he had missed the great chance seldom granted mortals. For a moment he had the feeling it was over, that the waters would come. He waited but nothing happened. Only the tree crickets beat their throbbing night pulse into his ear. The town remained. The silent streets and sidewalks of old Unionville continued to lie undisturbed around him.

Down Wington's hill he knew he had a place of refuge still to go to, the house of her in whose companionship he had felt the nearest to his mother after she had died. He descended Union Street, past the smell of ancient straw from the old stables at the alley, past Leshers' butcher shop. As he turned the corner under the big Lesher ash trees he could see ahead the outline of the house that was his second home.

The family tale had it that his Great-Aunt Teresa had once owned the large valuable lot on Kronos Street at the corner of Union. Wily Chester Troutman, national head of the P. O. S. of A., had persuaded her to trade it for his smaller and less valuable piece of ground on Back Street. On her lot he had built a huge three-story brick pile topped by a cupola, and on his lot she had built this modest yet substantial home in which John Donner had been born. It still belonged legally to Aunt Teresa, but was known as Aunt Jess's house, and Aunt Jess paid the taxes.

The old man stood across the street drinking in the intimate scene, the remembered red brick walls with their white woodwork and green shutters, the side lot encircled by a fence of wire-enclosed pickets he had once helped Uncle Dick to paint green. In the soft gloom he could make out the small-paned windows of the pleasantest basement kitchen in Unionville, the Maiden Blush apple tree whose fruit he hadn't liked too much, and the small, roofed side porch with a long French window leading into the parlor, a porch with two facing white benches sweet in May with locust blossoms. Soft yellow light flowed from the sitting-room windows above the basement kitchen, and red light from the hanging hall lamp through the transom over the front door.

On the front porch he had to restrain himself. Why, he had never knocked on this door in his life, or rung the bell, but tonight he turned the crooked handle and waited.

By the slow answering sounds that came from far within the house, and by the long time required for an answer, he knew who was coming. Already through the door he could feel her presence, a big woman filling the narrow hallway beside the stairs, bearing up powerfully over her "game" leg, rising up and down on one side as she went, like the side-wheel drive of a locomotive. It was a painfully slow gait for a boy to slacken himself to on the way to church, no more than a mere crawl, but he had often done it. "Wait for the halt and the blind," she would say playfully, or in the house, "Will you run upstairs for me, my love and my dove? Your legs are younger than mine." Her smile at such times was light, little more than a momentary movement of the facial muscles. But to outsiders she would smile gaily and poke fun at her affliction, telling the story of the Pennsylvania farmer who on meeting her with his buggy at the station had greeted her with, "My stars, but you're lame!"

It's lucky that Jess has a sense of humor, her friends said. The group around her at Church Guild was often the liveliest and her "take-off of grand opera," if she could be induced to "perform," the high point of the evening. She would seat herself reluctantly at the piano, lay mute hands on the keys as if getting into the mood for some prayerful opus, then go off into a burlesque of wild soarings and passionate tootlings you would never suspect from so noble a face and bearing, all the while giving her voice a very elaborate and intricate running accompaniment on the piano. She could play the most difficult music on sight. Cousin Rose, who had a salon in Vienna frequented by the great of her time including Brahms, had told Aunt Jess she could be making her thousands instead of pennies had she gone to Europe to study. But Aunt Jess had married Dick Ryon instead, a gentlemanly Irishman, a railroad conductor when he worked, and had supported him most of her life, giving lessons to the stubby young Pennsylvania Dutch fingers of town.

Not that she ever bit the hand that fed her. She received

her Pennsylvania Dutch neighbors like old friends, which they were, in her kitchen (they would never come in any other way), asking their advice on cooking, gardening and money matters, careful to be "common" as they. The only admission she ever made of a difference in their stations was to her own friends and family when she would use their pronunciation. "Are you very bissy?" she would ask ceremoniously in calling, or, if one of her friends used language not befitting a lady or gentleman, "Now Pappy Graef. You better behafe!" invoking the name of a local church pillar. She had a whole vocabulary of her own. Once she heard an exaggerated pronunciation from parlor or pulpit, she never forgot it. "Pleazaunt" and "experiaunze," both accented on the last syllable, were two of her favorites together with "d'yew" and "juty," reminders not to take too seriously what at the moment she was saying.

Now the door opened and there she was as he remembered her when a boy, the deep lines he knew so well already forming in her face. Many the time he had seen her go to the door in an apron. This evening she had on a somber black dress with glittering black beadwork, her hair done up severely, her face grave.

"Yes?" she said as to the veriest stranger.

He had to work hard to control himself. He wanted to cry out, "Don't you know me, Aunt Jess?" He dare never do that. He must be wary.

"I guess you don't remember me, Mrs. Ryon?" he said.

She looked him over carefully with those keen eyes. His heart sank. Her face never changed. Were there no vestiges of his youth remaining?

"I can't say that I do. Should I know you?"

"I met you once when I was younger," he explained.

"I meet a great many people," she told him. "My father was a minister."

"Yes," he said. "I know. May I come in and talk to you a little?"

A shadow crossed her face.

"I was just about to go out. My father—Reverend Morgan—is to be buried tomorrow. Perhaps you can come some other time."

"No," he said hoarsely. "I might not be here some other time."

"Well, I'll be sorry to miss you," she said formally. "But I must go. I'm late now. Next week if you happen to be in town, do come and see us."

Politely she began to close the door. Alarm rose in him. He

couldn't let her do that. Why, she had been his favorite aunt. She had always welcomed him as one of her own, had been mentor and encourager, filling his ears with stories of the "family," including the Scarletts, the good ones, the bad ones but all cursed or blessed with "the Scarlett mind." As a child it had embarrassed him, made him want to escape. But when as a young man he had tried to write for publication, she had stood by him like a rock. "Charles Appleby Seibert writes," she told him authoritatively. "He even writes books. If he can, so can you. You're his cousin." Never did she say, "He is our cousin." It was always "you," although she was closer to him than he. Not only his worldly but spiritual welfare had been her concern. "Whatever happens in life, you must always love Jesus," she would remind him. Even when he was a child it had struck him as unreal that Aunt Jess, gay, spirited, almost irreverent one moment, could be so pious and religious in another.

He played his last card.

"Won't you let me come in just for a minute and talk to you about Johnny Donner?"

"Johnny?" she repeated, widening the door. "What about Johnny? He isn't in trouble?"

"All of us get into trouble sooner or later," he said.

"But he's only a boy!" she cried. "He was in here not twenty minutes ago." Her eyes suddenly stormed. "I don't know what you are trying to get at, but I won't thank you for coming here and trying to run down our Johnny."

She started to close the door again, now firmly in his face, and would have done it if an unmistakable cracked voice of another day and age hadn't stayed her.

"Jessie, who is it? Somebody to see me?"

"It's nobody to see you, Aunty. Who it is I don't know except that it's nobody who's very much." Then Aunt Jess shut the door.

It was almost immediately opened and the caller saw peering out at him his Great-Aunt Teresa, poetess, teacher and "lover of children," grimacing in what was meant to be a welcoming smile, a woman in her eighties, her flesh eaten up by the vitaminless years until all that remained was an impression of hair, bones, skin and glasses. She reminded him of nothing so much as a scarecrow from the fields done up in castaway clothes and somehow living and breathing. He remembered how she would run off from the house in those ancient clothes, humiliating Aunt Jess. Even in her last year or two when she was virtually dying, she would escape like a wayward child, sally over town and countryside, her once active and sparkling mind now lapsing. But she never forgot a tribal face and stopped most every man, woman and child to tell them accurately enough what family they belonged to and some anecdote connected with the clan, preferably bringing in her father, a squire, soldier and hotelkeeper for many years, who knew all the dark secrets of the community. To listen to Aunt Teresa, he had practically won the War of 1812 singlehanded, and Brother Timothy had saved the Union against the Copperheads. Her memory was prodigious. She could still give in detail Brother Timothy's debate with Vallandigham in Springfield, Ohio. Her causes were numerous, her defense vigorous. He remembered how embarrassed he was as a small boy to find her in the alley he had passed tonight, protecting drunken Mike Whalen from a gang of yelling and stone-throwing boys, calling down the wrath of God on them and counseling the great brute of a tramp to overlook their infamy. The pair had made an unforgettable picture on his young mind, the lady and the beast. What particularly shamed him was that Aunty had worn no skirt, only an old red flannel petticoat. He looked

down now and found she had the same garment on today.
Well, he reflected, she had probably come to his rescue tonight much as she had Mike Whalen's, out of pity for the
downtrodden.

"Come in." She grimaced. "You know, 'Come in the evening or come in the morning. Come when you're looked for, or
come without warning.' " She peered at him. "I wondered
how you were and what you have been doing."

He tried not to look at Aunt Jess as he made his way down
the hall after Aunt Teresa into the sitting room, to be swallowed up in the past, in a distillation of feelings, slow time
and the genes of mortality that few houses have today. It
was as it had always been, the yellow oak chairs and buffet,
the deep windows, the cubbyhole closets and the door that
led out to the children's schoolroom. There were the same
smells, of old leatherbound books, of cigar ashes, of the
Rayo lamp and from the kitchen below. On a chair by the
lamp sat Uncle Dick, thin, stiff and faintly contemptuous as
ever, the *Evening Bulletin* that had come on the six-o'clock
train up defensively before him.

"Be seated," Aunt Teresa said, as to her charges in school,
and when the old stranger had slipped down to the stool he

had liked to sit on here as a boy, she beamed. "Low-seated and high-minded! How is Palmyra? Why isn't she with you?"

Uncle Dick lowered his paper to glance significantly at Aunt Jess.

"She thinks he's your father!" he said.

At Aunt Teresa's words, John Donner had felt a queerness pass over him. Somebody had recognized him, given him a place in the family at last. He answered gratefully,

"I haven't seen her for a while, Aunty. But I hope she's all right."

"This isn't Pap-pa, Aunty!" Aunt Jess raised her voice. "Pap-pa is dead. He died Wednesday morning. Don't you remember? He's to be buried tomorrow."

"Elijah dead!" Aunty cried. "Why didn't someone tell me?"

"We did tell you," Aunt Jess said. "Many times."

"I must go to Mary," Aunt Teresa declared, rising. "My poor sister!"

Aunt Jess caught her.

"You can't go to Mary. She's in the cemetery long ago. Palmyra is Pap-pa's widow. You just asked about Palmyra."

"Of course I know Palmyra," Aunt Teresa said stiffly. "How is she?"

"She's good as can be expected," Aunt Jess told her. "You saw her. You were up to the parsonage yesterday. You talked to her."

"Certainly I've talked to her," Aunty said. "I knew Palmyra when she was Postmaster Williams's daughter in Lebanon. She was a worthy enough person but nature hadn't eminently fitted her to be a minister's wife like Mary. She doesn't have the common touch. Mary was like Father. Father, everyone said, could talk to the highest or the lowest. To the lowest like a friend and to the highest like a king. I can still hear him when we had the store before he built the Mansion House. His voice would rattle the tinware on the ceiling."

Uncle Dick shook his head. He had heard the story many times before. He went back to his paper and Aunt Jess took Aunt Teresa by the hand.

"Now I think you should go up to bed, Aunty. You're tired. You took that long walk over Birds Hill today. Come along. I'll see you to the stairs." They disappeared slowly into the hall, where the caller could hear Aunt Teresa protesting she hadn't brought her book. In a minute she was back in the sitting room looking with surprise at the caller.

"Why, Elijah! When did you come? I wondered where you were. And how is Palmyra and the children?"

Aunt Jess hobbled laboriously into the room. Her eyes "looked daggers" (one of her own expressions) at the caller as if he were the cause of this trouble.

"It isn't Pap-pa, Aunty," she repeated. "If you look at him closely you'll see he looks no more like Pap-pa than the man in the moon." She gave a triumphant glance at him as if to say, I hope that settles you. Taking Aunt Teresa by the arm, she got her back to the hall again. John Donner heard her rapping on the door to the other side of the house, and he knew she was calling Sally Houck, who would go upstairs and stay with Aunty till she was asleep.

In her feathered hat and worn black silken coat Aunt Jess appeared again at the door.

"I'm going, Dick," she said and paused, her eyes hostile on the caller. "But first I think this man should tell us what trouble he claims Johnny is in."

"He isn't in trouble yet, Mrs. Ryon. Not until the future."

She groaned, a trick of hers he had forgotten until now, a horrendous sound of protest and ridicule with which she greeted anything preposterous. As a boy he had thought it amusing. Today he felt its sting.

"What would you say if I told you that I knew Johnny's future?" he asked.

"I'd say you were cracked," she said tartly.

"Please, Mrs. Ryon. You can help me!" he begged. "You may even help Johnny although you won't know it. Just talk to me a little about him. Tell me what faults he has, what mistakes he may have made that would make him want to come back here someday."

"Johnny has no more faults than the average boy and far less than most," she informed him.

"What about his liking to take walks by himself? Watching birds, he says."

"I think he's lucky to be happy in his own company." Aunt Jess was withering. "Most boys and men I know don't go watching birds. They're birds themselves—blackbirds. They have to flock with other blackbirds. They can't stand being alone. Now, women are different. They have their housework. They get used to being alone. If something happens to their husbands, they can fall back on themselves and have something to occupy them. But boys have no housework.

They have to run out with other boys. Men go to work with other men. When they come home at night, they have their wives for company. If something happens to her or if they retire, they're lost. They don't know what to do with themselves. They've never learned to go it alone."

Yes, John Donner thought, in the end every man and woman has to go it alone.

"But there must have been something," he insisted. "Something when he was young. A disappointment perhaps that left a scar. Or something he passionately wanted and never got."

Aunt Jess groaned again, not so deeply and dreadfully as before, but enough to carry her disgust.

"Every boy that ever lived has disappointments. Johnny less than most. He has as good a mother and father as there are in Unionville. He's the first boy in town to get a bicycle of his own. His father went to Philadelphia to buy it wholesale."

John Donner didn't hear her. Something in his own words remained in his mind. Could it possibly have been something not in him but in his mother's experience, something she had passionately wanted and never got, a wound which before birth or in their close sympathetic relationship afterward had been transmitted from mother to son? The old feeling about his father came back to him, and he remembered now certain clues in his mother. Scores of times he had looked up and found her staring into space, her sewing quiet on her lap. "What is it, Mamma?" he would ask and she would come back to the present. "Oh, nothing, Johnny," she would say, give him the tender smile he knew so well and go back to her sewing. What troubled her she had never revealed, but he recalled now that the poem that affected her most was "Maud Muller," the last words of which were, "Of all sad words of tongue or pen, The saddest are these: 'It might have been!'" Suddenly for the first time these things and his own doubts about his father came together, and they fitted perfectly. Ask! Ask! something inside of him kept urging. You'll never have the chance again.

"I wonder, would you tell me something, Mrs. Ryon?" he began. "Do you know or could you tell me if there was someone else Johnny's mother cared for before she married Harry Donner?"

Aunt Jess's eyes opened.

"That, sir, is none of your business."

"But it is my business," he insisted slowly. "Although I can't explain. Someday Johnny might want to know who he is."

"He is Johnny Donner," she said.

"I know that's his name. But is he really a Donner?"

He saw incredulity, then indignation, on his aunt's face.

"I don't know what you mean, but if you mean what you are saying, then you have the gall of an ox to come in this house and ask insulting questions. I'll have to ask you never to show your face here again."

"Aunt Jess!" he begged her.

"I am not your Aunt Jess," she told him witheringly. "And thank God I never will be." She stood there for a moment, a picture of magnificent wrath and contempt. She glanced at her husband. "You can be tolerant to him as you like, Dick Ryon. I just hope to heaven I won't have him to contend with when I get back. Now I'm going." With great dignity she limped majestically out of the room.

There was no other sound except the slow ticking of the clock until the front door closed behind her. The caller was aware of his Uncle Dick's eyes on him, dark, distant, a little annoyed and with something else around the mouth he couldn't quite name.

"You took her at a bad time with the funeral tomorrow," he said coldly.

"I'm sorry," John Donner said.

His Uncle Dick leaned forward and the something the other couldn't quite name turned into a kind of amused weakness under the mustache.

"You said, or at least you gave the impression," he began, "that you believed Johnny's father wasn't Harry Donner. Do you have any basis for that statement?"

"Nothing anybody but I would understand," the caller admitted.

Richard Ryon whistled.

"Well," he said sarcastically, "you certainly jump in with both feet where angels fear to tread."

John Donner wished he hadn't spoken. Why had he? All he knew was that in this house he felt very close to the secret and mysterious source, as in the old game when they called out, "You're warm." This was where he felt "warm," where he had been brought into the world, the house he had been coming back to all his life. His father's and mother's house had constantly changed, a few years in a parsonage here, a few years there. Aunt Jess's house had stayed the same.

He returned to his Uncle Dick. On the shelves above the

Rayo lamp were the first books of Florida he had ever known. He could still feel the sensation they had given him, of a primal land, of the strange Seminoles and stranger Everglades. There was one red book in particular that had left its flavor with him. He could still almost taste it, binding, paper, type and all. His Uncle Dick had sent it North when a conductor on Flagler's railroad that was then just reaching south of Jacksonville. His Uncle Dick had been there when most of the state was a jungle. He hadn't stayed long, but long enough to send up the first grapefruit ever seen in Unionville. Nobody had liked it.

"I wonder," the old stranger begged, "if you would let me go through the house."

His uncle's expression did not change, as if the request was beneath considering.

"We'd bring the old harridan out on us," he refused briefly.

"I once lived here and should like very much to see it again!" John Donner begged.

"Nobody ever lived here except the old lady and us," Uncle Dick informed him.

"It was on the other side. When I was a boy."

"Well, I couldn't show you the other side," Uncle Dick

said flatly. "The Houcks live there." He considered him with a skeptical eye. "You say you lived over there when you were a boy. I judge the old harridan isn't more than fifteen or twenty years older than you. She claims she built this house when she was forty. So when you were a boy there was no house here at all."

"It was in another life and world," John Donner explained.

At the look his uncle gave him, he knew it was the wrong tack. He better not get himself in deeper. He sat very still, tasting while he could the invisible emanation pouring from the old honeycomb of a house. That door with the heavy wrought-iron lock, they said, had originally opened to steps in the yard. Now it led to the bare schoolroom where Aunt Teresa had taught her kindergarten, usually with an apple on the Baltimore heater to "purify" the air, and a pair of stools up in front of her desk so she could question two pupils at a time. Under the schoolroom was the dim outer basement, with Uncle Dick's blue bicycle in a corner, with crocks on the shelves and bare hard earth underfoot except for the brick walk to the door. Under where he sat now was the basement kitchen with its two red cupboards, the stairs coming down, the low bridge of a whitewashed rafter, and the windows lifted back in summer on long wire catches. Here you looked out level with the ground outside, an experience that as a boy turned him into a creature no higher than a cricket, intimate with grass and grasshoppers. The other door led to the cellar, musty with the smell of spoiling potatoes, earth and coal, of a hanging safe and of a red bread tray on sawhorses.

Emotions were fast crowding now. What had happened in this cellar, he never knew. There was talk that his Great-Grandfather Scarlett had once murdered a peddler in his Mansion House cellar uptown. John Donner's mother and Aunt Jess had ridiculed the story, but as a boy sent for coal at Aunt Jess's he knew terror till he was back with the throated bucket from the Nameless Dark to the warm secure kitchen, with the octagonal steel kettle simmering on the stove, and his mother and Aunt Jess telling stories over the red cloth.

He heard a movement and looked up. Uncle Dick had got formally to his feet and stood there waiting with Northern Irish dourness. It came to him with a little shock that the man had had enough of him and wanted him to go. He wanted to get him out before Aunt Jess returned. He wanted to get back to his paper, Uncle Dick who had once been his friend, had looked up to the young writer, tramped the hills with him while he talked of the West and the stubbornness of these Pennsylvania Dutch farmers sticking to their stony hills when they could homestead the rich level soil of the West.

The stranger got up reluctantly. He felt abandoned and confused.

"If the young could only know," he apologized for his uncertainty. "But then they wouldn't be young any more."

There was no reply. He feasted his eyes for the last time on the Scarlett sofa, on the cubbyhole doors, on the yellow buffet that Aunt Jess used for papers and such, on the rug whose pattern was like the face of an old friend. In the hall he kept peering up over the banister. How well he knew what lay beyond. How many times had he raced those stairs, his hand never touching the rail!

"Could I go up for a minute? Just in the hall?" he pleaded.

Had he said it or hadn't he? Uncle Dick did not reply. It was dim up there but he could see the open door to Aunt Jess's bedroom, could feel the very shape of her bright red bureau with its bits of veneer missing, the still brighter red blanket usually folded at the foot of the bed, the polished window board that raised level with the sill. You could sit on the bed and play solitaire looking out at the Machamers next door. You had to go through Aunt Jess's bedroom to get to the back bedroom which had been added to the house when the schoolroom was built. The floor slanted like a ship's deck in a storm so that as a boy sleeping in this room with Matt he had the pleasant feeling of being adrift at sea. The front bedroom at the other end of the hall was Aunt Teresa's, a severe, anciently furnished cell with grim ancestors looking down from the walls. He had stayed away from that but by day and night he knew the attic. He had been sent there to sleep when the house was full, once as a small boy with Polly. He remembered waking in the middle of the night and reaching out to touch his sleeping cousin, curious to find out how a girl's flesh felt, since he had only brothers. She must have been nine or so, and he five or six.

He felt his face grow cruel with ties and memories.

"I wish I could see Matt and Polly," he said.

"Supper over and they're gone," Uncle Dick told him. "The devil knows where."

John Donner listened. They weren't here. The house was silent.

He scarcely moved, consuming every minute, hoping the absent might come. At the door to the parlor he halted. There was no light except from the hall but even in the gloom he knew every object intimately, the black marble fireplace that carried through to the sitting room, Aunt Jess's tall frosted-glass parlor lamp painted with blue flowers, the brass sconces on the wall that she had promised many a time should go to him when she died but never had, and the dark hulk of the piano. It was the piano that next to Aunt Jess he had felt closest to in this house, the carved Chinese monster, half idol, half alive, the pedals its feet, the gnarled and broken jacks, as Aunt Jess called them, its fingers, the golden rods and the hammers that struck the strings its arms. Most alive of all was its voice. The hard tight treble sang very clear. The deep bass reassured that the foundations of the earth were still standing. He had hoped when he came down the street that there might be a child taking lessons, the pleasant background of faltering humility and industry. He could still pick up books that he had first read in Aunt Jess's house and hear along with the taste of words and smell of the paper the sound of Aunt Jess's piano.

He wished now he had asked her to play for him before she went. No one else had her "touch." He would know it anywhere. Once when he asked she would have smiled with her particular kind of half-make-believe pleasure. In later years she grumbled that her fingers were stiff as pokers; she couldn't play a note. Sooner or later she would go to the piano all the same, seat her bulk dangerously on the tipping, creaking horsehair stool, run her hands up and down the keyboard to warm and limber them up, shake her head with disgust from time to time, although those double and triple runs were like the wind blowing first one way and then another. He had once asked her how she did it, and she said, "I don't. They just go." Sometimes she sat for a while as at a bowl washing her hands, tasting the water, throwing up tinkling and rippling drops until satisfied. "Now what do you want?" she would say and if he'd brought her a new Schirmer book, she would page through it on the rack, swiftly picking out the meat, sampling snatches of this and that, making pungent comments like "That's clever, Johnny, very clever," or "The dumb jack. What did a grown man waste his time putting that down for?" When accompanying a singer she could and often did transpose to a more vocally comfortable key as she went without a moment's hesitation.

She had a weakness for Liszt.

"Poor man," she would say. "Rose told me he could play like an angel. But he's no composer. He just improvises like I do, perhaps better, perhaps worse if I haven't anything on my mind. Listen, how he keeps trying this and that. It doesn't please him any more than it does me, so he cuts some capers to cover it up. I never know where he's going and neither does he."

And yet her nephew noticed that she played Liszt almost more than anyone else. She even looked like him, the same powerful artistic face, the arched nose, the spirited way she held her head. Then suddenly she would turn and smile at you as she played, and your heart would melt for her and for those small hands that could somehow span more than an octave. Who could have foretold, John Donner thought, that those fingers which galloped so gaily and effortlessly over the piano should be found at the age of seventy-two, gnarled and worn like the keys of her piano, locked on the counterpane while she knelt on the floor by her bed in death?

"Oh, Aunt Jess!" the old man cried to himself.

But Aunt Jess was no longer here. She had gone to the house of the dead. Now he followed her out of the beloved place into the night.

CHAPTER FIVE

The Breeding Marsh

John Donner stood on the sandy sidewalk after the door had shut out the light. Aunt Jess's house still hung in a cloud around him, rich and warm with those intimate details once taken for granted, or of doubtful beneficence, but now enhanced, made sweet to the point of pain by the long past and the present still denied him. Actually, there's no house here, he said under his breath to comfort himself. All this is really gone, departed, old stuff, no more than some unaccountable figment of the brain. But even as he said it the house continued to stand there with its rectangular yellow eyes regarding as an alien him on whom it had once smiled as a friend, and in the end he felt that he was the old stuff, the departed, the figment of the past.

He reached out a hand to the third maple, the one over the gate that used to turn such a faithful vivid scarlet in the fall while others on the street reached no more than orange or pale cerise. He would prove it an illusion and hence all this unreal, fanciful. But the tree was a rock, the bark rough, knotted and insoluble.

If this were real, then he must be the unreal, he told himself, the insubstantial and imaginary. More than once in the past he had had this curious feeling about life and its illusions, coming on bits of evidence such as, for instance, his name. How often and incredulously as a boy and even as a man he had repeated it to himself, "John, John, Johnny, Johnny!" It had sounded strange and hollow to his ears all his life. He couldn't believe the name quite his. It never looked right, spelled with a "j" and with an "h" where no "h" should be. There was something wrong about it. He had gone over other boys' names, trying them, speaking them aloud, fitting them to himself. There were nearly a dozen that sounded more real, one in particular that he felt was really his, but in the midst of it someone would brutally call "Johnny!" and drag him back to the dream that others called reality.

He had once told his mother how he felt. She had confessed to him that she had never liked her own name, neither Valeria nor Vallie. He had felt better at once. He could tell anything to his mother. She was never surprised, or if she was, she didn't show it. Whatever his doubts about justice and right, about doctrine and orthodoxy, whatever shocking words or still more shocking conceptions he had heard, whatever his protests or questions, she had had them before him or had at least known about them. Her calm could lay so easily the specters in his mind. She was incapable of being outraged when he was concerned. She would not be outraged by him today. She had always understood him even when most irrational and incoherent. She would understand him now. He could not imagine her otherwise. She would listen no matter how grotesque and improbable his tale or how his father stood back. If ever she should not—but he dare not think of such an eventuality.

Deep in his mind he knew that this, hidden and concealed by a multitude of complex acts and thoughts, was what he feared the most, was why he had not gone to her already. Her heart was the one sure and priceless possession he could count on here in the abyss and dare not be risked or gambled. And yet eventually he knew he must do just that. He had best go to her now while the chasm still held and the water held back.

He went down the dark path his father's feet had taken under the great ash trees which grew so rank in Unionville.

Not until he was in his sixties had he learned that they were sacred among the ancients. He thought he could feel them like leafy idols over his head tonight, listening to his step, watching him without eyes, aware of his whole past. This was where he had played soldier with a wooden gun. And here under the biggest tree on Kronos Street, that some said had grown gross from human phosphates washed underground in the old hollow from the cemetery, was where as a child he had first noticed the changed track of the sun, that in October it was already dark at six. Beyond this tree he was setting foot in the home square, another very long square, the middle so far from lampposts that the gloom of foliage overhead confused him. He was uncertain whose house was whose. Only his feet knew, taking him unerringly to the steps they had run up so often and blindly as a boy.

Old and stiff, they wanted to run up now. The red hall lamp (all the best houses had them) was lighting him home. Another moment and he could burst in that old friend of a door, be young Johnny Donner and be safe.

"Careful! Careful!" he warned. He must go slowly, feel his way, knock on his own door like a stranger, but not on the front door lest his father come with a face that asked, "What are you doing here?" Around back there was a chance his mother might answer. There in that moment at the door together, recognition would come. Now what was the cowardice that still smote him as he made his way back through the familiar alleyway, and why should he have to struggle like a worn-out swimmer through heavy seas? There was light in the kitchen as always, a light soft and mild, and somewhere young people's voices.

His hand shook as he rapped on the door.

"Who's there?" a voice called, not his mother's. She never called like that. It was Annie, his mother's old Dunkard maid.

"I'd like to see Mrs. Donner." His voice was shaky.

"What do you want with her?" Annie demanded. The old stranger in the door gave the ghost of a smile. That was like Annie, only a midget of a woman (they used to call her Half Pint) yet always speaking her mind. What business did a man, and especially a strange man, have at this time of night with a married woman like Mrs. Donner?

"I just want to see her," John Donner told her. And when there was no reply: "I'm related to her."

"Oh!" Annie said, which meant several things—so that's how it is and why didn't you tell me before? "Well, she's not here. She's up at the preacher's." Then she added, "If you came for the funeral, you don't need to count on sleeping here tonight. She already has more than she can handle. I got to sleep with young Timmy."

So his mother was at the parsonage. He might have known. It was the family get-together the night before the funeral, with Uncle Peter and Aunt Hetty and all the great-uncles and -aunts from Philadelphia. He could never face his mother among so many. He had always had her to himself when they talked.

"Annie!" he begged.

"What!" she answered in the explosive Dutch intended to admonish or cow.

"Annie. May I talk to you a little?"

"Well, talk then!" she told him shortly, making no move to open the door.

"I can't talk through the cracks," he protested, turning the brown knob. His mother almost never locked the door, but Annie—a little fighting cock of a woman afraid of neither man nor spook, she claimed—would turn the key, he remembered, whenever she was alone.

"Why can't you?" she came back unmoved.

"Annie!" He shook the knob. "Let me in."

He could see her through the window standing small and

belligerent in the middle of the floor, her small white Dunk-ard cap on the back of her head.

"What do you want in for?"

"I want to see you and talk to you. I want to see the house again."

"You're not coming in here," Annie informed him. "Not till I know who you are."

"You know me," he promised. "You know me well. Don't you remember Johnny?" Why, as a small boy Annie had taken him everywhere.

"Johnny who?" she wanted to know. He saw her take the light and come to the window. She put up the shade to the top with one hand and with the other held the lamp close against the pane. A long-forgotten childhood feeling went over him at sight of the old green print of her dress, of the cocky nose and the small mouth turned down.

"I never seen you before, old man," she informed him.

"But you did!" he pleaded. "We were thick as thieves. You were very fond of me. You'd do anything for me."

"Well, you should of made hay while the sun shone," she retorted. "I don't know you no more." She put the lamp back on the table.

"Annie! You can't do this to me!" he cried.

She turned on him.

"Why don't you come in the daylight?" she scolded. "What do you come at night for like a thief trying to sneak and slobber your way in where you have no right?"

The old man stood silent. That had shaken him. What could he say? It was the great riddle. He could only answer that this was the way it was. There was no use trying to explain to Annie. After a little he turned and went defeated to the street. As he stood there looking back at the house such yearning came up in him that he could scarcely stand it, a yearning for many things vanished, but most of all for what as a boy he had valued so little and almost despised.

He found himself presently moving up the street. Once upon a time he had thought that man had invented nothing better than town life on a warm evening with the feel of neighbor friends around you, with the south wind stirring the town leaves and the lazy twang of frogs from the canal. The silent shadows of toads hopped in the garden. Occasional townspeople would pass on the street, the girls in light summer dresses, and all the time the drift of voices from front porches where families sat with occasional words be-

tween them or to those passing and pausing to chat and tell
some news, so that by the time one went from Mill to Maple
Street a social evening could be passed.

John Donner was conscious of them now, the mysterious
disembodied voices of the unseen, the immediate ones sub-
siding at his approach and resuming when he had barely
passed. "Who was that?" he could hear them ask. He tried
to conquer the alien reception with a hearty "Good evening,"
as he remembered his father doing, but although they replied
dutifully, there was reservation in their voices and he could
still hear their speculation after he was by.

He missed the fortifying sound of Hoy's blacksmith shop
as he passed it, closed for the night. The grimy bare and
muscled arm on the anvil might have put a little iron in his
veins, he thought, as it did for those who heard it day in and
day out. But if it had been open, he would not have gone in.
The street, that was for the stranger, for the unrecognized
and unbidden. He passed the Knittle house built, they said,
of bricks brought home in the Knittle dinner pail, two a day,
from the brickyard where Oscar worked. Next door was the
Ditrich house put up in canal days with a roof slanting much
farther back than in front. All the boys at school had looked

up to Eddie Ditrich, whose uncle wrote him letters from the Richmond jailhouse.

And now he was approaching the Swank house. Out on the West Coast on nights of winter rain he had more than once smiled over Emmy Swank, who in the early days boasted of one of the few bathrooms in Unionville but used the outside privy to "save the toilet." Even on snowy nights they could see her go out the garden walk with a lantern. Now as he came closer he heard the raw voice of the totally deaf who talk constantly to conceal their handicap, halting tonight only when the stranger was almost abreast and then loudly before he had fully passed, "Who was that? I thought it walked like Harry Donner but it wasn't stout enough. They say he's going to be a preacher, at his age!"

Oh, he told himself, the whole town was a living museum of people and places the like of which, once gone, would never be seen again. Back on Kronos Street, for Mifflin ran only to the school, he passed the shop of Dummy Noll, who had frothed at the mouth at young Stan Greenawalt, for taking him to be soled a pair of tattered shoes found in the canal. They were always baiting Dummy. Uptown was another deaf-mute place, Kissawetter's, like a scene out of Grimm's fairy tales, especially around Christmas, with roly-poly dolls rocking silently and toy figures mutely nodding and the proprietors, man and wife, making signs to the customers and the customers making signs to them until it seemed that the entire store and its glittering contents and all who came in had been put under a spell until the fairy prince should come and set them free.

The combined jewelry and clothing store of Jimmy Pomeroy next door was another place of necromancy and magic, black magic to a small boy of the church, the fearful dummies in the shadows, the row of forbidden books by the arch agnostic Robert Ingersoll on the shelf, and behind the counter the gaunt black-garbed figure of Jimmy himself, a watchmaker's magnifying glass glued to one eye, a ready and sonorous polemist who on Sundays walked the streets alone, absorbed by his grand thoughts, seeing almost no one, his face turned up to the heaven which church people said he was doomed never to see. Tonight John Donner remembered that a few days before he died Jimmy had written with soap on his bedroom mirror, "We fade and flutter at the end like leaves in the fall." He felt a kinship for the man tonight, a desire to sound out his philosophy but a customer turned in ahead of him, and he went on up the street past the wooden steps to the feed store of Georgie Brandt, who had tippled too much at the hose house one night and woke up next morning to find he had bought Trot Maurer's barber shop. Georgie couldn't barber but he had got Trot to stay and barber for him, and when Trot went home for dinner Georgie would leave feed to his wife and come over to get a customer ready on the chair till Trot came back, lathering him and talking, till one day Trot didn't come back and at the end an angry customer tore off the bib and put Georgie on the chair, lathering him till Georgie talked him out of it, for Georgie was a good talker and most people liked him.

John Donner tried to laugh at the memory, but the laugh wouldn't come, neither then nor when he passed the Daubert house, where young Cora and Jack had taught him the art of burping, swallowing air and storing it in the stomach until it could be belched out at will. One time in the midst of their accomplishment the doorbell rang and running to answer it they found Mr. Krammes, the Evangelical minister. He told them solemnly that Mr. Burlap, their next-door neighbor, had just died, and there the three of them stood helpless, not daring to speak or answer a word for fear of releasing a chorus of resounding belches.

Couldn't he ever smile any more, John Donner asked himself, not even at Chippy Luckenbill? Here was his Union Hotel across from the new tannery. The same Mr. Krammes preached against liquor and Chippy told his wife, who went to the Evangelical church, that if she ever got Krammes to preach his funeral sermon, he'd rise up in the coffin and curse him. In due process of time Chippy Luckenbill died and Krammes was to preach the sermon. Chippy's cronies and customers came to the funeral to see what would happen.

"Well," the church people taunted them afterward, "did Chippy rise up in his coffin?"

"No," his cronies said regretfully, "but he got mighty red in the face."

There must be something the matter with him, John Donner told himself, that even Chippy Luckenbill left him unmoved. He remembered he had had no supper. He turned downtown toward the DeWitt House, nearly as old as the town itself, with white verandas upstairs and down and a rich scent throughout of well-aged kegs and bottles such as survives in no bar or cocktail lounge today.

Inside the swinging slatted door the room was dim and cool. A few men sat at the far end with Jake DeWitt, last of the DeWitt line.

"Good evening," John Donner said courteously and stood at the bar.

One or two of the men mumbled but Jake did not get up. He had usually refused to do that for a single customer. The talk in the dialect went on and John Donner waited until in time another customer entered and Jake came reluctantly from his corner.

"I wonder," the old stranger said, "if I could get a sandwich and a glass of beer."

"Supper's over," Jake told him. "Dining room closes at six thirty."

"I know," John Donner said, remembering that meals were early in Unionville, dinner often at eleven and supper at four or five. "But I've walked pretty far and am a little shaky."

Jake's eyes still refused him, harder now, disapproving of the resort to pity. The other went on.

"Mrs. DeWitt was always a friend to me. Will you ask her if she'll feed a hungry man?"

Jake was examining him minutely now.

"What's the name?" he wanted to know.

"Donner."

"You related to Harry?"

The stranger nodded and Jake moved to the second customer, setting out for him a glass and the schnapps bottle without asking what he wanted. Then he turned, went into the hall and John Donner thought he heard him on the stairs. He came back without saying anything. It was a good sign, John Donner judged, and in time came a light rapping on the hall door. Jake was again sitting in his corner, but he got up at once and went to the door. The old man at the bar saw a pair of eyes scrutinize him intently from the crack. In a moment they vanished but Jake brought back a plate laden with a huge slice of homemade bread cut in half and stuffed with baked country ham. Then Jake drew him a heavy glass schooner of beer and picked up the dollar bill he laid down.

"We use good money here," he said, giving it back.

"What's the matter with it?" John Donner protested.

Jake took another bill from the till, laid it grimly on the bar, and the stranger remembered he was in the chasm. Beside the other bill, his own looked small and inadequate.

"It's good," he insisted. "It's just the new size."

"Too new for me," Jake grunted. "You can tell whoever made it he should use more paper."

"How much do I owe you?"

"A dime for the sandwich and a nickel for the beer."

John Donner reached in his pocket, relieved to find the solid hardness of coins. At least silver had kept its shape. He wished he had more of it. Laying a quarter on the bar, he left. When he came out, the street had changed. These were the same houses but the shape of roofs and walls appeared to have altered, as had the lineal relationship between doors and windows. Things he had forgotten until now came flooding back to his consciousness. Ahead waited the broad, shallow Kunkel house, where the skeleton of an infant lay at this moment hidden in the thick walls and not to be found until they were dismantled. Across the street with a slate roof and many stained-glass windows stood the ten-room brick house of Harold Sterner, who was to sell tannery stock among his neighbors and friends before bankruptcy.

The walker could smell the new tannery now as he went down the Methodist church hill. Across from it lived another tannery owner, whose wife and eight children, John Donner knew, were within the decade to die of tuberculosis. Passing, he could see some of them tonight through the bay window, Mrs. Bambrick, a gracious woman, reading to three of her younger children. They made a disturbing scene, the blond

hair of the girl down over her shoulders, the boys too young
and fair for death. There had been a time, John Donner
grimly remembered, when he wished he might have knowledge of the future.

Oh, the town was shot through with things now he would
give a great deal not to know, tragedies that cried tonight
to be halted before it was too late. He put down his head as
he passed the bitter house where Helen Easterly had taken
her life some four months after John Donner as a boy had
seen her with three older boys lying in the straw of her
grandfather's stable. And there was the house where Alice
Seltzer had her girl child in the dead of night, never to see
her again. Before daylight they had taken the babe twenty-
five miles by horse and buggy to the Lebanon hospital, from
which she was adopted by a country couple to be brought up
in the Amish faith and never to know that her father and
uncle were one.

Certain houses almost cringed as he passed, but the sor-
riest, most wretched and hopeless of all was the frame cottage
of the Flails. John Donner himself at the age of ten had
come with the curious to see the blood still dripping into the
tiny front room while upstairs in two still smaller and more
accursed rooms lay huddled shapes that had once been Griff

Flail's wife and four small children, struck down in their sleep by the father, who had then dispatched himself. It was a masterly job by an experienced hand, for Griff was a butcher for Sherm Rhine, and the nearest neighbors during the night had never heard a sound.

As John Donner approached the tragic little house tonight he could see the soft lump of Mrs. Flail, still alive, with two of her younger children, one rocking in her arms, the other at play at her feet. Concern for them swept him, and he halted at the rail.

"Go away!" he cried, his voice thick. "Leave Griff. Leave him tonight. Go home. Don't risk another day or it might be too late."

The answer he got was horrified silence. He saw that the mother had snatched up the second child and was staring at him through the dusk, while neighbors started up from their porches to see who was threatening a poor woman and did she need help to save herself and her small children from a madman?

Perhaps he was mad, he told himself, expecting others to listen to his ravings. He escaped uptown, but he felt debased. In youth or even manhood walking was a joy, effortless, almost an act of flight, but given age and weariness the walker was aware of its grotesqueness, to be cut in two below the waist and able to transport yourself about only by setting one of these severed parts in front of you and then the other, and so on monotonously like a tadpole split down the middle imagining itself king of creation.

Everywhere he went now he thought he tasted a strange bitterness in the air as if the unhappy Unionville dead released by the hour were abroad in the town, trying like he to find solace on the streets where they had walked before, leaving trails of melancholy and despair. He puzzled over the deep insupportable sadness. Were he and the dead the only victims or did many of the living feel it, too? At this very moment here in Unionville were there those who went about their chores and errands, confessing nothing to those about them, saying "It's a warm evening" or "See you tomorrow," carrying their grief with them to their beds and to their feet when they got up in the morning, never knowing its source, nor did any other man?

Some of the stores were closing but the depot remained open and lighted, waiting for the eight fifty-five from Auburn, the last train till the early miners' train in the morning. John Donner was grateful for the open waiting room. He felt a little peace here in this house that belonged to an absentee landlord and was free from the pressures of the personally occupied. Nobody resented his presence or showed that he wished him to leave. The very look of the benches was impersonal, meant for transients such as he and the two old men smoking and talking with long lapses of silence in this pleasant retreat shot with the scent of travel and far places and the sudden chatter of the telegraph instrument.

Sitting here, John Donner thought of the stations of the cross. Well, there were also stations of the aged and out of work of all ages, sanctuaries in which to catch their breath and pass that which lay such a daily burden on them. As a boy he had never thought much about it, but he could see the stations in his mind now, all over Unionville, the watch box at the crossing, the stools in Rehrer's saddlery and at the shoemaker's, standing room at Hoy's blacksmith and wheelwright shops, the chairs on the DeWitt porch and store benches under the wooden mercantile awnings, a dozen facilities now vanished. And yet modern towns considered themselves humane and all-providing.

He watched with regret the train come in, the sprinkle of passengers and the two old men depart to their homes. Never had lighted windows looked so desirable and unattainable, even those far back from the street. As a boy he had

thought the peculiar and withdrawn lived there. Tonight the
gloomy paths leading to these distant houses were gilded
with golden light. Their windows and those of all Unionville
houses, he noticed, had a mysterious and elusive quality like
life, not artificial and glittering as the electric-lit windows
he had left above the chasm. Down here they flushed with a
soft bloom, as if a glowworm had turned on its cold light.
You looked for it to go out but it kept on and you kept
watching it like a modest flower or small miracle. Almost
never did these windows plunge suddenly on, or off into
blackness, like lamps fed by the fickle magnetic spark. They
dimmed and faintly brightened as if even the inanimate here
breathed and was alive.

Everywhere he wandered now the smell of the river pursued him, soft and seductive, like the scent of a woman fol-
lowing him, reaching out and touching him, till at length
he turned and submitted, crossing the lower tracks, passing
Christenson's coalyard office, another station of the aged, and
Felty's Mill, which he had always thought the best-propor-
tioned building in town. The black mouth of the covered
bridge known as Felty's opened before him. Entering, he
could taste the dry smell of ancient dust and make out
through the gloom the great double arches rising on either

side. He remembered how in the Red Bridge as boys they would climb the whitewashed arches and lie hugging the wood while a train roared through, shaking the structure as if to demolish it and them all.

He felt his way up the south arch here, a triple one of great planks from the early forest, steamed, bent and riveted together. At least he would have a roof over his head. It wasn't too bad stretching out on his wooden couch, feeling the massive strength of his bedstead, hearing the low twittering of fellow lodgers about him, grateful for a high open place to look on the dim world outside. A mist was rising from the river, obscuring all the familiar forms and landmarks, shrouding them in an impenetrable veil. Even the stars were hidden. Well, the old must steel themselves to the obscuring of familiar sights, become resigned to an existence in mist and veil. The pueblo Indians of New Mexico were wise to build their houses of earth, to become accustomed to dwelling in the clay of their final resting place.

Lying there, he heard the sudden cry of terror from a bird in a nearby treetop, then all was still. Had it, he wondered, been picked up in the talons of a feathery flying beast, carried off God knows where as dark shapes rise at night from the abyss to do the same to men? John Donner kept thinking of the birds as he lay there, the peril of their common nightfall. Small wonder they sang in the morning but why did they also at approaching night?

The river made mysterious occult gurgling noises beneath him. He remembered it shallow enough here. The older men said that a ford had preceded the bridge, and yet the sound was deep, black, stirring with nameless imaginings.

"Never cross water," a palmist had once told him.

He would not cross it. He just intended to stay here suspended over it. If he did not sleep, keeping vigilant, waiting for daylight, he would be safe.

CHAPTER SIX

The Confluence

When the man awoke he did not know at first where he was. Troubled sleep had confused him, taken with dreams of a bridge that men had to pass through. It was a dark bridge, very late at night, and the men were nearly always alone, most of them on foot, reluctant, talking incoherently to themselves to brave them into the black unknown. Only one had been in a hurry, with a horse and buggy that rattled the plank and stirred the dry dust so the dreamer could taste it in his throat. Now the dreamer lay remembering, seeing again in his mind the shadowy figures, hearing their lonely voices, feeling the threat and sadness of that bridge, and the chill of the river it spanned. The chill was still in his flesh and his bones when he awoke.

Gradually the dusty ax-scarred rafters and black-stained shingles overhead took shape and brought him back to reality. With stiff joints and muscles he came backward down the wooden arch. Once down, the tender town scene through the telescope of the bridge revived his spirit, the red tin roofs of the remembered streets, blue summer woodsmoke rising from the lazy chimneys, the familiar odd shapes of Unionville houses half hidden in the fog of leaves, the green hills lifting beyond and pink clouds hanging over them, all simmering and asleep as if in an early-morning spell. He stood drinking in the delicate perishable picture, then descended the path through rank-smelling weeds to wash his face in the river.

All the way up Mill Street with no sidewalks and very few houses he noted the vagaries of the ambient envelope here in the eddy behind Shade Mountain, the unseen layers of cool and warmer air, the winding currents of some elusive scent now gained, now lost. Distillations of hearty old-time breakfasts, of frying ham and potatoes, pursued him. His fingers felt the thin change in his pocket. He must go hungry or unshaven today and the latter was unthinkable if he wanted to look presentable to his mother. God knows that his best would be lacking enough.

Joe Heisler's barber shop already at this early hour held faces and heads to be readied for the funeral. Sitting on the long bench were Rob Felty, the miller, Charley Hartman, the station agent, and Sherm Rhine, the staunch friend of and moneylender to his Aunt Jess, but neither they nor Joe acknowledged his presence after the first glance. Only the eyes of the customer reclining under the razor watched him covertly through the mirror, secure in his turned back and lathery disguise.

Sitting back at last in the leathern chair, John Donner saw the old mine boss from the west end of the county pass the window. He had had a stroke, lost his family, and come down off Broad Mountain to the DeWitt House to board. Daily, summer and winter, he could be seen dressed in the same lightweight coat and trousers, never an overcoat, exercising his bad leg, a tall, gaunt, alien-looking figure moving painfully but persistently up and down Kronos Street. The man had become a resident of Unionville some years before he died and yet had remained almost unknown, an outsider and intruder. They called him "the foreigner."

That's who he felt like, John Donner told himself, as he left the barber shop, his shaven skin sensitive to his home street after so many years. He hadn't realized how gratefully the darkness last evening had shielded and covered him. At the Eagle Hotel he turned back to the alley and pursued its secluded way downtown, stopping only by his grandfather's red stable. It was dim inside but he could make out through the open half of the stable door the black tail and bay rump of a horse. The old man unhooked the lower door and stepped in.

The beast turned his head and the great dark orbs observed him. It was Mike, the old retainer, whom Pap-pa had kept so long. As a boy John Donner had played in his stall, climbed on his back, ducked between his legs, had thought this horse wiser than most men, a beast who could tell the time of day. The afternoon mail came to Unionville at four in the afternoon. If Pap-pa returned to town after this time, the horse went to the post office and stopped. If earlier, Mike went straight to the stable.

The stranger stepped into the stall.

"Mike horse!" he said, giving the old childhood name, and the aged beast buried his muzzle in his arm.

So another besides Aunt Teresa knew him. Standing there in this frequented place, under the cobwebs laden with dust, with the furry ears so close to his face and the distinctive horse scent in his nostrils, John Donner half expected to see his dead grandfather come from the house, lowering his head to protect his stovepipe hat at the stable door. Pap-pa kept three high silk hats, his best for church and funerals, the second best for rainy weather, the third for garden and stable.

"Mike, do you want a drink?" he would ask in his sharp metallic voice. If Mike whinnied, he was thirsty and would drink. If he shook his head and you gave him water, he would turn the bucket over impatiently with his nose.

Twice while John Donner was there Mike lifted his head to whinny. He did it again after Morris Striker had come to curry him.

"He's been doing that ever since old Morgan took to his bed," Morris said. "I guess that's the way it goes when you get up in years like you and me. We keep looking for people that can't never come around no more."

John Donner left through the parsonage yard. Things were still as he recalled them, the curious high narrow board-walk, the rich black powdery soil, the greenish privy called "the outhouse." The parsonage and church looked ageless, the vegetable garden neglected. Pap-pa had been the best gardener in Unionville, his mother said, raising the earliest lettuce and never tasting it, saying slyly that he didn't belong to the ruminating tribe. Here were the octagonal wooden pump, unused since water had come to town, and the summer kitchen, on the roof of which his young mother, Aunt Jess and Uncle Peter used to dance in their night-dresses when Pap-pa and Ma went out in the evening. Today the summer kitchen buzzed with activity and cooking smells but the green blinds of the house were pulled down.

When John Donner came around to the front gate he found Kronos Street filled with activity. From Union to Maple street it had been roped off, and neighbors had set out benches and kitchen chairs for the country folk. Inside the ropes it was clear of vehicles but farther down, as far as he could see, horses and buggies, carriages and spring wagons stood end to end along both sides of the street. At the church a steady human stream already flowed through the iron gates and up the stone steps to the front door. The old stranger in the coal driver's coat had trouble getting to the church proper. They tried to shunt him into the Sunday-school room downstairs, filling up now for the overflow service.

It was a little shock for John Donner to find himself again in his father's and mother's church, as if coming back to a bit of the stone age, the grim ancestral Unionville faces, the rigid backs of church worthies up front, the unmistakable Ira H. Smather family seated in their family pew like boul-

ders embedded in their glacial hill. The ancient high red
plush chairs on the pulpit platform might have been from
Moses' time. The design of painted leaves on the wall behind
the altar were horseshoes upside down. The baronial silken
purple cloths on the pulpit furniture still hung embroidered
with IHS that Timmy had once thought stood for Ira H.
Smather. But the organ sounded slow and wavering. Could
that be the instrument on which John Donner remembered
his Aunt Jess playing such magnificent Bach, sitting like a
priestess at her altar? A strange woman sat there today.

The older church members, the visitor recalled, hadn't
liked the new colored windows, wishing for the ancient
frosted panes. John Donner had disagreed. The stained glass
sparkling with color had been a refuge from his grandfather's sermons, especially the tedious morning sermon in
Pennsylvania German. He had passed much time in their
bright world. The pink lamb, the white dove, the feathered
angel, the harp, the scroll, the beards and rich robes of the
apostles, the green hills of Judea and the blue water of
Galilee had all been boon companions of his Sabbath youth.
His favorite was the purple grape and he had often supped
on it until dinnertime. The names of donors lettered below
were a roster of the pillars of the church. He thought the

colored pictures their personal choice and property. Of an early summer evening service, the western window "to the memory of Mary S. Morgan" sometimes flamed with crimson and gold as befitted his grandmother in heaven at thirty-nine.

Many times had he heard the story of her death. He sometimes thought that he, as yet unborn, had been present in person. He could see it so clearly, Pap-pa standing like Lincoln at the head of the bed, young Aunt Jess and Uncle Peter at the foot, and his mother, the littlest of the children, held up to see her mother die. She had been carried upstairs by Cousin Vic, a junior at Gettysburg College, who in less than a year was to follow with galloping consumption taken on the football field. It was a grief-stricken hour for all save the chief participant, who sat propped up in bed, her cheeks pink with pain and fever, glassiness already in her eyes, crying out triumphantly that she was going to heaven that day and would see Jesus. Grave, bearded Dr. Sypher sat on the edge of the bed holding her wrist. Twice he begged her to take a little brandy but Mary Morgan refused, saying she wanted to go to God and the Saints with her mind clear and all her senses intact.

That had been some thirty years before—ninety years to

the nineteen sixties—and now her husband, who had acquired
a second wife in the interim, lay here in his extraordinarily
long golden-oak coffin by the altar rail under the lectern and
pulpit he had read and preached from for more than forty
years. Sunday mornings, they said, he had had a habit of
looking keenly out over his Bible to see who was missing, and
God help those who were not sick when he called Monday
morning. There was the story of Katy Gangloff, who saw
him coming and hid under the bed in the front room of her
log house, telling her son what to say. When he answered the
door he said dutifully that his mother was over the mountain.
"I see, I see," Pap-pa had said dryly, looking at the pair of
shoes sticking out from under the bed. "Well, next time your
mother goes over the mountain, tell her to take her feet
along."

John Donner guessed no one would tell that story from
the pulpit today. They would tell the more pious ones, how
Pap-pa was known to preach with a child in his arms, omit-
ting that Pap-pa disliked crying children in church and had
instructed mothers in the congregation to let their very small
restless children free on the floor, with the result that the
aisles and occasionally the pulpit crawled with tiny tots,
which was why he sometimes in self-defense chose to pick up

a baby playing around his feet and hold it with one arm while with the other he emphasized his customary "hence we find."

There was a stir on the jute-carpeted stairs. The preachers were coming, a whole troupe of them in their black garb, the local clergy followed by important men of the church including John Donner's Great-Uncles Howard and Timothy, noted preachers and joint editors of the denominational weekly, preceded by the president of the synod with Uncle Peter's friend from the big Lebanon church, then the bearded head of the Evangelical Lutheran Church in America walking with the smoothly shaven president of the seminary at Gettysburg. Uncle Timothy, the brother of Mary Scarlett, marched with his face up, an aristocratic man with a sharp commanding nose. Aunt Jess said he had once ordered a servant woman with a wash basket off the Philadelphia streetcar in which he was riding. Uncle Howard tramping beside him would never have done that although Uncle Howard's wife was a Bartlett from New Hampshire, descendant of Josiah who signed the Declaration of Independence. Uncle Howard wore a slightly raised shoe on one foot and when he walked moved up and down, which gave him a kindly aspect.

In their wake as if shielded and comforted in their ecclesiastical presence came the mourners, Uncle Timothy's
and Howard's wives, Aunts Martha and Frederica, support-
ing between them Pap-pa's second wife and widow. The
stepchildren and grandchildren called her Ma. All the
women were heavy from forehead to feet with veils and
mourning. Great-Aunt Eugenia, after whom Gene had been
named and who was supposed to have been a bit wild before
being married off to the Rev. Charles Woolston, couldn't
come from the great distance of Colorado. Right after Ma,
as if to protect her if she faltered, walked a composed Uncle
Peter, Pap-pa's only son, an almost jaunty younger clergy-
man who wore a sweeping mustache of uncertain color to
give his bright and merry face a little gravity. With him
were his wife, Aunt Sophy, a doctor's daughter, who considered herself superior to the Morgans and whom they never
liked, and the three children, including Myra, the oldest of
Pap-pa's grandchildren, a tall, proud, willowy girl with a
tremendous pompadour of pale shining hair. Aunt Jess followed in unaccustomed black veil with Uncle Dick, very thin
and stiff. John Donner never remembered seeing him in
church before. With them came Matt and Polly and Aunt
Teresa, who looked more skin and bone than ever in her an-

cient and rusty black bonnet drooping with strings and ornamented with what looked like black beetles.

The old stranger had sat rigid in his back pew and now he could hardly contain his emotion as he caught a glimpse of the womanly figure he knew so well, the large bones, the fairly long thighs that made such a wonderful lap to a child, the ample shoulders and breast he had cried on. But that certain face, so erect and restrained with others while warm and eager to him, was hidden under long black veiling so he could see nothing except the form, like the outline of a memory whose living heart and breast were still barred from him. She moved up the aisle quietly, driving ahead of her the three boys while his father, strong and powerful as always, brought up the rear. Having ushered them into their proper place, he took his seat at the edge of the aisle, vigorous and alert as if to protect them from the contagion of death and all its malignancies.

Oh, Dad, let me be with you! the old stranger in the rear begged. For a few moments something in him strove desperately to be sitting up there at his accustomed place with his brothers and parents, beloved, guarded over and secure. In the end, repulsed and shaken by the impossible, he came back to his battered self.

The service was very long, the singing by the middle-aged choir quaint to his modern ears. Uncle Timothy and Uncle Peter's preacher friend together with the local clergy had left to conduct the overflow services, one in the Sunday-school room, the other in the open air in front of the church, but there were plenty of clergymen left up here. Now, why did preachers look so grim and bloodless in their black dress, their faces fixed as the wooden tops of the tall pulpit chairs they sat on? Through the prayers and readings, each by a different speaker, and the funeral eulogies, all mixed with similar sounds from the other two services, John Donner escaped as when a boy through the open pane of the stained-glass window to the fresh greenery of a tree outside. The world out there was still young, the golden light about it very close to that which later shone in the face and voice of his father when he repeated certain passages with mystical fervor. "Now unto him that is able to keep you from falling," and "Grace be unto you and peace from Jesus Christ our Lord" and "To the only one God, our saviour, be glory and majesty, dominion and power, both now and ever, Amen."

Sitting here among ecclesiastical shapes and symbols, with the strong stone walls of the church about him and the repetitions of faith in his ears, he marveled how pure that emotion from his father could reach him, letting him see how the church might appear not to himself but to the devout who attended year in and out, who here prayed their prayers and confessed their creed, whose families had belonged for generations, who were born, bred, baptized and raised in its shadow, who enjoyed the favor of its ministers and dignitaries, and to whom church, altar, pulpit, Bible, choir, sacraments, clergymen and synod were familiar furnishings of another, richer home, while the brother churches of its denomination were a chain of celestial forts here on earth, so that dying in the faith was almost as being borne into the nations of heaven.

The service ended and the congregations from the other two services began to file in a bottomless line up the aisle and by the altar to have a last look at the marble face of their old pastor. Those in the upper church were the last to join the queue, and in the end John Donner had to go along like the rest, past the bier and out the door, leaving the family and clergy alone with the body. He was hardly down the stairs when the first clang of the bell startled him, certainly no strange sound, for he had heard it often and never outgrown his fondness for its deep vibrations quivering on the air. Even on Sunday the slow turn of the immense wheel was evident. Whenever he had come back and heard it again so deliberate and timeless that for a moment after each turning one almost believed it had ceased ringing, he thought he knew why most Unionville men preferred not to leave home. But the sound today was something else, the stroke of a man with a hammer, a cruel, barbaric, almost brutal finality to life and hope that reached to his very bones.

There was such a swarm of people outside the church that he could scarcely make out his mother, just the crown of a woman's hat as she came down with the family before getting into one of the carriages. As a rule the people started off at once on foot for the cemetery. The services at the grave those days were the crowning act of a man's life, like the other Elijah going in a chariot to heaven or the town drunkard let down on ropes to eternal hell. But today the crowd remained filling street and sidewalks. John Donner soon saw what the people waited for. They were watching old Mike, a black ribbon tied to his bridle. He stood hitched to Pap-pa's buggy in front of the hearse. He had turned his head now to watch the pallbearers bring out the long yellow coffin and load it on the hearse. Afterward, Morris Striker said the old horse started off on his own with the empty buggy. Morris was supposed to lead him by the bridle, but he merely walked beside him, and Mike led the procession, turning up Cemetery Road from Kronos Street without guidance. Ma always said she had never heard Mike neigh from the stable again.

The foot procession formed quickly now, two by two, flowing in a human stream, at first beside the carriages, then swinging out into the middle of the street behind, a long, winding, almost endless tail of Union Vale humanity. Walking along with it, John Donner remembered what his cousin Georgia, who spent most of her life in Europe, had told him. "I always said I wanted to be in London when Queen Victoria died and in Unionville when Mr. Morgan died, and I had to be in Italy both times."

By the time the old man got up the hill, the press was so great around the grave he couldn't get near. Once or twice the breeze brought a snatch of familiar words, "I would not have ye ignorant, brethren," "In the evening it is cut down and withereth," and "O death, where is thy sting?", then the wail of the choir, who in those days marched summer and winter up the hill to raise their voices over the grave without benefit of organ or pay, sending the traveler with hymn and lament to the other shore. It was more pagan than he realized, John Donner told himself, closer to the Greeks. As a youth he had thought it criminal to torment the bereaved with mournful words and dirges. The feeble efforts to disguise evil with the words, "Asleep" and "At rest," carved serenely over pits of corruption had angered him. Now that he was older he wondered if he might not have been too thin-skinned and refined. If you had friends and neighbors to climb the hill and raise well-meant words over you at last, why should you prefer paid strangers consigning you to earth or fire?

He saw finally that the services were over, the multitude dispersing, life withdrawing to its warren, leaving the dead to the dead. Until the crowd was gone, he wandered among the narrow lands of the departed, noting long-forgotten names and the oft-chiseled melancholy words, "Father," "Mother" and "Our Darling," far from home and warm bed in this chill stony place. The phrase "He is not here but risen" aroused in him as always an inner rebellion. "Just the same, God," he spoke grimly, half aloud, "Thou hast missed a wonderful bet if it isn't true." What he meant was that the Infinite had overlooked a chance to delight itself and confound the wisest of men by showing them how little they knew, how man was a great deal more than he guessed and creation far beyond any sensible and reasonable conception.

Wasn't it curious that now at this gloomy time he should think of some of his grandfather's funeral stories, especially the one about Manny Keefer, typically Pennsylvania Dutch. He told Pap-pa that when he died he wanted to be buried north and south instead of east and west like everybody else in the cemetery. He didn't want to have to get awake and sit up to see the sun shine in his face on resurrection morn. He would sooner sleep. That was something he had never had enough of. For thirty years he had had to get up at three o'clock in the morning and walk four miles to town to catch the early miners' train. He was tired and if resurrection came before he got rested, he'd be "grichlich." It was a long entertaining story full of Manny's talk together with what his wife said and what Pap-pa and the grave digger said. John Donner seemed to see and hear his grandfather telling it now with his unreadable face and those peculiar motions of his long arms to relieve his inner enjoyment.

The carriages and most of the crowd were gone back to town when John Donner started to follow. Near the cemetery gate boys were playing, leaping over tombstones, rolling and tumbling on grassy graves, seeing nothing frightening in this calamitous place. One of them looked up and noticed him.

"There's that crazy old man that hollered at Mrs. Flail!" he yelled.

The cub pack came after him hooting and jeering. In the cemetery there was little to pick up and throw but once they came to the road, shale pebbles showered after him. He remembered how he had seen Mike Whalen trying to maintain his dignity under attacks like this. Aunt Teresa in her red petticoat had been of more help than he thought.

"Aunty! Where are you now?" he cried.

CHAPTER SEVEN

The Source

He felt a little shaken when he got downtown. His tormentors left off here but a few shale fragments had found their mark and drawn blood. He stared at the sight of red rubbed off on his hand. Well, anyway, he was not an insubstantial figure of the imagination. He was real. He could bleed.

But now that it was over he felt singularly faint. He noticed that only a few of the teams on Kronos Street had gone. Horses buried their noses in feedbags or in corn-stained wooden boxes. Most of them were farm horses in blinders with the motherly look of a farmwife with glasses whose work was never done. Up the street he found country folk sitting out on the benches and chairs provided in the roped-off square, open baskets by their feet, the younger ones crowding the curb, most of them with fried chicken in their fingers. This was a holy day set aside for the funeral of their spiritual ruler and pastor, a day like Sunday in which "thou shalt not do any work, thou, nor thy son, nor thy daughter, thy manservant nor thy maidservant, nor thy cattle, nor thy stranger that is within thy gates." At the same time, having paid their respect, they meant now to take advantage of their holiday, enjoy these unaccustomed privileges, talk with relatives and friends, laugh and joke, for the solemnities were over and behind them now, buried like the corpse and not to be exhumed.

"You can't live with the dead," John Donner had heard them say more than once when a widow or widower remarried within the year. And the first remark when one of their own died, hardly waiting for the last breath, was often a matter-of-fact "You got to think of the living now."

Standing by the church, he could hear above the murmur of dialect a sound of rushing like the wind in the trees. It was weakness, he told himself, a lack of food. But he thought the roaring in his ears grew louder and on the end knew it for what it must be, Kronos rising in its banks. A kind of terror seized him. Strange that these country folk did not notice. Perhaps they did not want to hear it. They would never believe that where they stood at this moment was to be buried beneath tons of flood and ooze.

The sound of chaos was plainer now. He remembered he had not as yet got to the heart of the great secret. He had not even spoken to his mother or heard her voice. He had not seen her except at a distance blurred by the impenetrable veil.

He made hurried steps to the parsonage yard. At the open window he could hear them at the funeral dinner, his grandfather's table extended by every board, groaning with meat and potatoes, jarred fruits and vegetables, with pies and cakes, with sweets and sours, not a sad occasion but a celebration of victory over life and the grave. He could hear his great-uncles holding forth at the table, striving to be heard above the other, not on their deceased brother-in-law. Due praise and ceremony had been paid him. It was time for the living now. Even Aunt Jess could scarcely get a word in and he didn't hear his mother try. She would brood most over her father's passing. She was the youngest, his favorite. The story went that he would let her as a small child play with his hair, sit patiently with his head down thinking about his sermon while she braided the long reddish locks with her tiny fingers. One Sunday evening the church bell had surprised them and not till the congregation snickered at him in the pulpit did he realize that his hair was still plaited. "You, Val!" he had said accusingly, shaking his long finger at her from the pulpit.

It had started to rain and John Donner pushed in the front door. Here in the hall stood his grandfather's huge hatrack hung with imposing high hats and other lesser head-gear. He felt the old parsonage atmosphere swimming around him, compounded of woodsmoke and books, of ink and paper, of black horsehair furniture and ancient objects and clothing smells not to be singled out but all contributing their scent to the heavy aroma. Presently he found himself at the dining-room door, and saw them all at the long table before him. These were his own people, his kindred. The blood in the veins of many of them was the same as flowed in his. Most of their forms and faces were familiar as the back of his hand.

Uncle Timothy's eagle eye flashed and saw him. His knife and fork went down and his head went up.

"What do you want, old man?" he called with authority.

The stranger in the faded coat and unchanged shirt felt like the unbidden guest at the feast.

"Excuse me," he said. "I was looking for someone."

"The name. What's the name?" Uncle Timothy asked impatiently.

"There's no name," John Donner stammered. "I just wanted to find my mother."

"Your mother, old man?" Uncle Timothy glanced across the table for confirmation of his raised eyebrow. "You have hopes of finding her at your age? Well, we can't help you if you don't tell us who you are."

"I don't know who I am," John Donner said. "That's what I'd like to find out."

There was silence and attention now around the table. He could see his Aunt Teresa, her face all bone and glasses, staring at him.

"Why, Elijah! Where did you come from? They told me we had buried you today." She half rose from her chair.

"Hush, Aunty!" Uncle Peter said, pulling her down. "It's nobody you know."

"But he said we were his dear people and kindred," Aunt Teresa insisted, although John Donner remembered saying nothing of the sort aloud.

"You better get him out of here, Peter," Uncle Dick advised.

Uncle Peter turned on the stranger his kindly and expansive charm.

"We're glad to see you and your smiling face as always, my friend. But we'll have more time to see you later in the day."

"Wait!" Aunt Teresa called. "He asks who he is. Do you remember my 'Ode to Phaethon'? Howard and Timothy printed it in the *Messenger* years ago." Here her voice changed to the high singsong tongue in which she intoned poetry.

" '*Deep deep in the hills the nest was made.*
Deep, deep in the hills the form was laid.'

"I think I can recite all twenty-two stanzas. It starts—"

"Not now, Sister, not now," Uncle Timothy said hurriedly. "We remember it very well." He turned to the stranger. "You ask who you are, old man. Your name I don't know but I can give you a text from Job. The twenty-sixth chapter, I think. 'He stretcheth out the north over the empty place and hangeth the earth upon nothing.' "

He gave a triumphant glance as if to say, does that settle you? but John Donner stood unsatisfied.

"You talk in riddles," he said. "My mother would never do that. Would you excuse her and let her speak to me in the hall?"

They exchanged glances. He could barely see his mother, hidden behind Uncle Howard's shoulder, but he thought he caught a glimpse of her warm concerned eye.

"Come back in an hour, my friend," Uncle Peter said. "We'll have more time to talk to you then."

"In an hour none of us will be here," the old stranger said. "We'll be gone forever, never to see each other again."

A murmur of protest, almost of horror, circled the table. All eyes were fixed on him.

"It's that cracked old man that came to the house last evening!" Aunt Jess broke the spell.

Uncle Peter pushed back his chair.

"I'll take care of him," he promised and scraped his way behind the chair backs, wiping his mustache with his napkin as he went. At the door he hooked arms fraternally with the old stranger and forced him gently but firmly down the hall toward the kitchen.

"Don't send me away," the old man pleaded. "Not till I see her."

Uncle Peter smiled his friendly benevolent smile under his scraggly mustache.

"Your mother isn't here, old man," he testified. "No matter what notion you may have in your head. You must take my word for it. We are rational Christian people. This is our own family. It's a solemn and affectionate occasion. We are together for a few short hours before going our separate ways. You don't want to spoil our grief with any untoward act."

"I must be going my separate way soon, too," the old stranger said.

"Are you hungry, old man?" Uncle Peter asked. "If you come along to the back porch, I'm sure the ladies in the kitchen can fix up a plate for you."

"No, thank you," John Donner said. He would accept no crusts from the back door of his grandfather's house as did Mike Whalen, Georgie Ellenbaum and other tramps, picking scraps from old plates on the kitchen step. He waited for Uncle Peter to exhaust his badge of kindliness, to be a victim of the Scarlett sarcasm that ran in his blood. Once as a youth John Donner had asked his Uncle Peter a favor. His father had sold Uncle Peter groceries at cost from the store, packing and shipping them in boxes and barrels with his own hands. Later when they had to sell his mother's sideboard with the claw feet to pay a bill, the boy had secretly written to Uncle Peter, who had a big church in Cumberland County, begging him to find his father a church paying more than four hundred and fifty dollars a year. His Uncle Peter's letter in reply had been all kindliness except for the final line, "Good-by, John, and remember to keep your nose clean!"

Now by the peculiar set of Uncle Peter's mouth under the mustache and by the forced kindly crinkling around the eye he guessed that the Scarlett sarcasm and rebuke were not long in coming. Before they reached the lips there was a movement from the dining-room doorway and Uncle Timothy appeared, unruffled and commanding.

"Let me handle him, Peter. You remember what Christ said, 'This kind comes not forth save by prayer and fasting.' You go back to your dinner and I will try to deliver him."

"I am one of your own flesh and blood!" the old stranger protested. "Look at me. Don't you see the family resemblance? They always said I had your nose—"

"Silence!" Uncle Timothy commanded, holding out two

imperious hands, palms upward, and John Donner remembered how Cousin Georgia in her seventies used to imitate
that word and gesture. She and her young friends, she said,
would be singing around the piano when their house guest,
"Uncle Scarlett," as she called him, would suddenly appear
from the library. "Silence!" he would call imperiously, and
when they reluctantly subsided would recite how he and
Aunt Frederica had heard Jenny Lind sing at Castle
Garden.

Georgia used to say that Johnny had also inherited his
restless pacing from "Uncle Scarlett," that the man had
worn a path through their library and dining room repeating
to himself, "It's all right, it's all right, it's all right, but the
bread is stale, stale, stale." What he meant they were never
able to decipher, for the table bread was fresh daily. They
thought it must have some mystical or religious allusion, and
John Donner used to wish he could remember the uncommon
old man more than his bearded photograph and the bold
handwriting in several books on his father's shelves, "Merry
Christmas to Vallie's boys from Uncle Timothy." Well, here
he was in the flesh to be seen and savored.

"Why don't you leave us in peace now?" Uncle Timothy

suggested. "You may come back and tell us your burdens later."

"I can't," the stranger said. "The waters are rising to cover us all."

"Water?" Uncle Timothy demanded, the Scarlett sarcasm in full flower in his lip. "Do you fancy yourself Noah called by God Almighty to save us from the flood?"

"No," the old man told him sadly. "You will never be saved, neither you nor Aunt Frederica nor Uncle Howard and Aunt Martha. Your bodies will be buried in three hundred and ninety-eight feet of water and all they'll ever find of you to take up to higher land will be a bucket of maggoty dust and a few shinbones."

Uncle Timothy drew back.

"You have a profane and irreverent spirit, old man. Why don't you go now and leave us in peace?"

"I will go then," John Donner said. "But not in peace."

Uncle Timothy insisted that he leave by the back door. He himself stood on the back porch to see that the visitor did not immediately return.

The ejected old man passed through his grandfather's iron gate. It was drizzling now but the sound of rushing water still deafened his ears. He must go to his mother's house before it was too late. He had seen little enough of it last evening.

For a long time he stood under the crisping fanlike leaves of the horse chestnut, saluting the old double house with its warm yellow clapboards. Intimate boyhood smells rose to his nostrils, the dank odor of bricks that seldom if ever dried out, the sharpness of sulphur from some kitchen coal stove, the musty scent of the nearby alleyway that never saw the sun. But it was the odor of wash water in the little gutters down the alleyway and across the sidewalk that affected him most, bringing back a long-forgotten memory of being carried back here as a child, from where he did not know, but suddenly feeling safe when they reached these certain reassuring smells of family and home. Inside of him something melted, tensions buried so deep he doubted they had been unknotted since he left this place.

He started up the front steps. It was the same old porch, narrow, shoe-scarred, without a break or partition between the two houses. He peered in the front window under the half-drawn shade. It was like looking into an old-time Easter egg at a scene so faithful and real he could almost step into it, the golden-upholstered parlor chairs and sofa, the silken-lined memento catchall on the wall, the framed engraving of the battle of Waterloo, the crokinole board against the arch and in the second room the mahogany-veneered sideboard with claw feet that had come down to his mother when Ma had brought her own furniture from the Forge.

He could hardly keep from pushing open the front door. Over the threshold would be the reddish Brussels hall carpet with an extra square on top for wear in front of the door; the lesser hatrack and umbrella stand; the cannonball door-stop that Pap-pa had picked up on Seminary Ridge at Gettysburg after the battle.

When he looked again, far up the street people were streaming out from the parsonage. It gave him a sense of added excitement and suspense. His family would be coming now. He became aware presently that he leaned against the house, that he couldn't stand erect, that he was slipping and couldn't stop. It was like something he had once seen old Carson Rarick do in his father's store. It had been the old man's ninety-third birthday and he had tramped over town with his crutches to celebrate with his friends. Now while leaning against the counter he had started to sink. He went down slowly, almost imperceptibly, smiling, without a sign of alarm or request for help so that no one held out a hand to stop him. It was as if he were doing it himself, on purpose, was tired of being on his feet and wanted to rest a little on the floor where he presently found himself, his head propped up against the lower part of the counter, still fully conscious, smiling and content as if it were the most natural thing in the world for him to be lying on a store floor.

John Donner did not go that way. He wasn't smiling and he felt himself losing consciousness. His last thought was relief that his father couldn't keep him out of the house now. He would be lying at the doorstep when they came. They would have to take him in. Then he must have blacked out, for he didn't hear a sound when he fell.

Shortly afterward he became aware of people carrying him with difficulty into the house. Even with his eyes closed he recognized the old-time presence around him. A great peace drifted through his veins. He was home at last, back in his father's house with his brothers about him and his mother at his side to take care of him and of every problem that rose, as when he was a child.

Then he opened his eyes and bitter disappointment seized him. He was still outside the longed-for place. The woman gazing at him with black eyes was not his mother but Mrs.

Bonawitz, pronounced Boonawitz in Unionville, their neighbor on the other side. For years she had done the Donner
wash.

"How do you feel now?" she asked sharply, as if he had
committed some uncalled-for act at her door.

"I must go," he said and tried to get up.

"Lay still," she ordered. "It's lucky my man stayed home
from the mines for the funeral. He's gone for the doctor."

"I don't need a doctor," he protested.

"Wait till he comes before you talk so big," she told him.
"My father fell like that when he had his first stroke and
he had to have the doctor till he died."

She went on relentlessly, telling him all the intimate and
depressing details of sickness, which, especially when fatal,
obsess the simple and primitive. His only defense was to
close his eyes as if asleep and not open them until he felt
a practiced hand on his wrist and looked up into the familiar
face of Dr. Sypher, bearded, calm and unreadable. These
were the same grave eyes that had watched his grandmother
and grandfather leave this world and himself brought into
it, not in the house next door but in the north front room
of Aunt Teresa's brick house on Mifflin Street. The doctor's

eyes were fixed away from him, on the face of his large gold watch in his hand. He pocketed it presently and laid his hairy head with its prophylactic drugstore smell on the chest. Then he sat back and gazed at his patient speculatively as with all the time in the world.

"Is there any house around here where you could be put to bed?"

John Donner thought carefully.

"No, sir."

"Nobody around Unionville know you?"

Yes, the stranger wanted to say, one did, an old horse, but he better not say that. He had been called mad already.

"I wouldn't like to ask them," he explained.

The doctor mused.

"If I let you go home, how long would it take?"

Home? Why, it would take only a minute. But no, the doctor must mean his other home, the one that seemed unreal today, clouded with mist and very far away, somewhere in the morning fogs of the Western Sea.

"I don't remember now," he put him off.

"Could we telegraph your family to come and get you?"

The older man kept silent. How could they do that? How

long would it take a telegram today to reach his family tomorrow? The house and street address did not even exist as yet. How could they ever find him here?

"What you ask is impossible," he said.

"Haven't I seen you somewhere?" Dr. Sypher asked. "Would I know your name?"

"I'm a Donner," the stranger said reluctantly.

The name produced instant reaction.

"Any relation to Harry next door?"

"Distantly," the old man murmured. "He doesn't remember me. I saw him at the store last evening." He felt his weak position, almost that of an impostor. "I'm a little more closely related to her."

"She was a Morgan," the doctor said. "I didn't know of any Donners on her side."

"Yes, there were three or four of us Donners related to her," the old man insisted. Then suddenly: "I wish I could see her. Do you think she would come?"

"Just how are you related?" the doctor persisted.

The old man sank back.

"It was such a long time ago." He closed his eyes. It was no use. It was all so difficult, complicated and painful to explain the simplest reality. He heard the doctor speak to Mrs. Bonawitz.

"You might ask Mrs. Donner. But I'm not sure he knows. He's pretty weak and his memory's affected. I shouldn't like to move him today. Could you possibly give him a bed tonight? He may come around and remember who he is in the morning. Then we can telegraph and get him home."

Mr. Bonawitz protested.

"She's had too much sickness already, Doc."

"You wouldn't put him out on the street," she said angrily, turning on her husband. "He reminds me of Dawdy. He was out of his head a little at the end, too." She turned to the doctor. "I'll keep him for one night."

With the doctor helping, they half lifted, half pushed and drew him up the narrow stairs. In the back room they undressed him, then pulled down over his head a starched nightshirt such as he had seen his father wear. They laid him on the rope bed and left.

He lay there quietly enjoying the clean sheets, listening to the rain on the roof, the slow drip to the alleyway below. He remembered as a small boy standing at the front window next door watching raindrops such as these exploding in a sidewalk puddle that wasn't really a puddle but a sea with waves, winds, a distant shore and Christ asleep in the boat. That afternoon he had gone with his brothers to paddle in the river brown with flowing soil, the water warm from its passage over the warm earth, the air rank with the smells of river and banks. Their clothes lay in a dry spot under the trees. It must have been soon thereafter he had lain sick in bed one day aware for the first time of the wide rain system advancing, the thickening clouds, the rain starting, increasing, the parched patches of hairy moss in his mind drinking and greening, the dried-out bogs reviving, the forest mold soaking, the bark of trees blackening and rainy-weather springs flowing. Ever after he had been a spectator of the cosmic forces bringing sea change to the dying earth. Why couldn't man, he wondered, observe so dispassionately the advance of other cosmic forces, those of the greater change, noting first their signals, then their approach, feeling their nearness, their presence, their strong arms not made with hands carrying him out of reach of the power of man's mind to know or understand?

The low ceiling here was exactly like the ceiling in the back room across the wall, sloping a little toward the rear, with the paper stained over the back window where water had once seeped in. But there were two beds over there. Gene and Timmy slept in the other and one night after he was asleep they had taken the shepherd's crook from the wall and "stirred apple butter," he being the kettle. Waking, he had tried to kill them, throwing with all his might the silver-lead rock Uncle Dick had brought from Colorado, missing them and mutilating his mother's picture, *The Wedding Procession* by Delacroix that she had got from Larkin's.

"It's the Scarlett temper," his father had said, although he had something of a temper himself without benefit of Scarlett blood. Uncle Howard said the Scarletts had been French, very sensuous and high strung, and Cousin Myra, who was ambitious, believed that they had noble blood, which was what made them so high-minded and demanding. She said she had heard of an old document in which the name was spelled Scarlatti. John Donner knew later that this was an Italian name. He suspected that Myra had been duped and sometimes doubted he had French blood at all, but he never doubted the Scarlett temperament and wildness, the sudden rush of desire to let go, come what may, to do the violent and forbidden. He remembered an overwhelming impulse as a very small child to jump on a moving coal train, and when a little older to "borrow" a neighbor's twelve-gauge shotgun to shoot quail he had seen crossing the road. He had begged, wept, demanded of his mother. The quail were in Mr. Ulrich's meadow right now waiting to be shot. She daren't stop him. The world would come to an end. Compelling pressure rose in him like flood water tearing at a dam. His will couldn't be thwarted.

His mother had understood. She knew just how to calm and gradually check him. He had seen the same fire at rare times in her, the head up, face alive, the usually calm gray eyes shining with the deviltry of some witty rejoinder or daring enjoyment. Most were agreed it came from the Scarlett blood but all had a different name for it. Aunt Teresa called it "the lambent flame of the Scarletts"; Uncle Timothy, "the Scarlett genius"; Aunt Jess, "going off on a Scarlett tangent" or, when she felt kindly toward the inheritor, "the Scarlett mind." "You've got the Scarlett mind," she had told her nephew after he had written his first book. He wasn't sure if it was irony or a compliment, and came to the conclusion it must be both, chiefly the latter with just enough of the former to keep him from getting a "swelled head." His mother seldom, if ever, spoke of the Scarletts. She just said "Mother" or "Grandfather" or "Aunty" and you knew whom she meant.

"Is there anything you want?" Mrs. Bonawitz asked suddenly, coming into the room.

"I'd like," he said in a low voice, "if I could see my mother."

"Yes, I guess all of us would," Mrs. Bonawitz told him.

"I'd like," he persisted, "to see Mrs. Donner."

"You asked that once before," Mrs. Bonawitz reminded. "If I see her in the yard I'll tell her."

"Will you ask her," he begged, "if she'd let me see the house? Tell her I've come a long way. Tell her I'd be very grateful. I wouldn't be any trouble. Tell her I used to live there once."

"When was that?" Mrs. Bonawitz asked suspiciously.

"It was a long time ago," he murmured, slipping back.

He could see rank disbelief in her eyes.

"Now you go to sleep," she told him.

He tried to do as she said, aware how dependent the old were on the younger, how they must submit, put will behind them, let things take their course. Through his dozing he could hear voices downstairs, first one then the other, sometimes mingling, going on and on, hers sharp, short, sarcastic, his deeper, heavier, ominous. It sounded like quarreling but John Donner knew his townspeople better. Once he had asked his returning Grandfather Donner, "How's everybody in Reading?" "I don't know everybody in Reading," his grandfather had snapped. And yet he had one of the softest hearts in Unionville. No tramp dare go away from his door hungry. John Donner's own father would sound angry and embroiled at a distance talking to the boy's mother at home. If in the midst of it the doorbell rang, he would compose himself for a moment, then go to the door singing a cheerful hymn to correct any wrong impression on the caller.

Just the same there was something in those voices, in the harsh Pennsylvania German tone and testiness, that aroused deep down in John Donner a kind of terror. It reminded him of something, something monstrous, of some other voice, one that gave him a feeling of indescribable fear and repulsion. Whose voice it was buried down there he didn't know. Perhaps if he knew he would know why he had come back and what he sought.

Lying there with closed eyes, he tried to find some clue to the identity of the frightener. He let the remembered horror hang over him, not too painfully, just enough to bring back figures and faces that moved through the back of his brain, shadowy forms, but he thought he recognized them well enough. He must have been very small the first time his

mother had taken him to the butcher shop but he could still
see the wolfish grin on the man coming out of the door who
told him, "You better watch out they don't keep you and
cut you up with the meat." For several years he couldn't see
meat chopped up without feeling his own thighs and breast
under the chopper with the thighs and breasts of the harm-
less beasts of the field.

He was a little older but not much when he went with the
other boys of his Sunday-school class to see Tuck Helwig
the day before his funeral. They didn't call it viewing then.
Something in him dreaded moving closer to the small active
body he had known so well, now lying cold and still in the
terrifying small white casket. When he shrank back, an old
man, probably not as old as he was now, had chided him in
the dialect, "Sei net so bong. Er schtinkt net." It wasn't the
rebuke but the coarseness to his young friend that troubled
him and to this day he couldn't smell the overpowering
sweetness of carnations without faint nausea.

Now other faces were floating into his mind. As a boy he
had found something manly in Pennsylvania Dutch outdoor men, like Cap Ridenour marching at the head of
Company C, Fourth Regiment, down Kronos Street in his
broad white stripes, or Guy Hains and Frank Grebble,

noted hunters, pigeon fanciers and dead shots, who knew every foot of the Shade Mountain. He had looked up to them admiringly till he went to a pigeon shoot across the railroad and saw Frank Grebble tear out the eye of a live pigeon before putting it into the trap, burning its rear hard with his lighted cigar so it might fly erratic with pain and be the harder to bring down.

But the face that hung darkest in his mind was that of the woman on Canal Street where you came down the bridge over the railroad, a dark dried-out face with eyes even blacker than Mrs. Bonawitz's, eyes that took hold of you like flypaper and wouldn't let go. Townspeople had seen her turn into a black cat and go through a knothole no bigger than your thumb. When old Mose Brant had shot his cow that wouldn't give milk, Dr. Sypher had had to pick shot out of Katarina Messer's buttocks. One morning her neighbor on one side heard her talking to her neighbor on the other. "I dreamt you hung yourself last night," she said to Mrs. Trumbo, who had seen much trouble, and two days hence Ray Trumbo, who lived in Turkeytown, had to cut down his mother from a rafter. Most of the young people hated to pass Katarina's house, especially at night or even in the daytime when they knew she was sitting at the window watching them. There was one way to protect yourself, the orthodox exorcism, "Kissmice," and hardly a boy or girl in Unionville who didn't say it aloud or under the breath and keep saying it religiously, "Kissmice, kissmice, kissmice, kissmice," until he or she was safely past and free.

The old man saw Mrs. Bonawitz come into the room with a yellow wooden tray. She propped him up with a heavy quilt folded behind the bolster. On the tray were greasy pannhas, which the uninitiated call scrapple, fried potatoes, plain bread and brown coffee boiled in the customary pot seldom emptied of grounds till no more could be added. He remembered what his mother would bring him as a child when bedridden, a soft-boiled egg, delicately browned toast and cambric tea.

"Feed me, Mamma!" he would say and she would put the sulphur-tarnished spoon with some egg to his wide-open mouth, this in compensation for being sick, giving him with each bite an indescribably warm shining look of the eyes.

"Now you got to eat," Mrs. Bonawitz said bruskly, "if you want to stay out of the bury hole."

There was the sound of a door downstairs and of voices, then Mr. Bonawitz's heavy tones in the dialect from the kitchen.

"I guess you don't understand Dutch," she told him. "When I was out back I told Johnny Donner you were related to his mom and wanted to see her. My man just called that Johnny's over now. I told him to send him up."

"Johnny Donner?" the old man asked, struggling to sit erect, his one thought how he would look.

She seemed amused.

"You don't need to mind. He's only a boy," she said.

He heard indistinct sounds in the hall below, then steps on the stairs, coming closer and closer, two or three treads at a time. Could it be, he wondered, that he had ever had a step so light and effortless? A boy rounded the doorjamb and stood in the doorway. His eyes fled from the strange old man to the woman.

"I told her, Mrs. Bonawitz. She said she couldn't make it any more today on account of the funeral and company but he can see her tomorrow." He said it quickly, almost as one word, and moved to go.

"Wait!" the old man called hoarsely and the boy turned with uneasy reluctance. Was it possible, the man thought, that he had once been slender, fair-skinned and light-minded as this, his blood vessels new and pliable, his eyes like spring water, his face fresh as a girl's? "Speak—say something!" he enjoined himself, then aloud, "How is your mother?"

"She's all right," the boy said as if with surprise that the old man would ask about her.

"Does she still bake your favorite graham bread and baked beans?"

"I guess so."

"You guess so?" the man said. "Don't you know? Don't you like it?"

"Yes, sir. It's all right."

"And the lamp in your room? Does she still keep it lighted for you at night?"

The boy stirred uncomfortably.

"Yes, sir," he said and started to turn.

"Wait!" the stranger begged.

He must be careful, he told himself. He daren't frighten him away. A hundred things he would like to say. Did he appreciate his mother, his youth? If not, for God's sake beat the ancient method of the zodiac, the slow unwieldy scheme of awareness after deprivation, the cruel system that taught you most beautifully and effectively when it was too late. On second thought, badgering would do no good.

You didn't learn the issues of life by being taught, threatened, reminded, coaxed. You could so learn the lesser arts and graces that never entered your real being but were a kind of mark on the forehead that gave you entrance to doors in life and in the end mattered nothing, like wooden beads on the abacus that never actually counted anything but zero.

What he wanted, he mustn't forget, was the secret, the final answer to the search. Now was his extraordinary chance. If anyone knew, it must be the child, himself, back here at the source.

"Will you listen, boy?" he asked hoarsely, earnestly. "I want to ask you something. Will you promise to think?"

"Why, ye-ss," the boy said uneasily, staring at him.

"Do you ever have nightmares? Don't answer me. I know you do. What I want to ask you is did you ever hear voices— after you're awake? I mean—that remind you of something, perhaps somebody in your nightmare?"

"I don't know what you mean," the boy stammered but there was fear in his eyes.

"You're surprised that I know? You needn't be. Just tell me something—have you ever had a notion whose voice it is?"

"No, sir," he stammered.

"But you don't like the voice?"

"No, sir."

"You're afraid of it—of the person?"

"Yes, sir."

"But you don't know who it is?"

"No, sir."

"You're sure?"

"I think I'm sure."

"Then sometimes you think you know?"

"No, sir," the boy said, but he whispered it.

"You mean you have no idea at all?" the man persisted. "You never had an idea who this person is? Not even the faintest idea? Not even now?"

This time the boy did not answer.

"Then you have some idea who it is," the man declared. He leaned forward, trembling violently. This was the moment of revelation. "You must tell me now who this person is. I command you."

"I can't," the boy cried and turned and ran down the stairs.

CHAPTER EIGHT

𝕿𝖍𝖊 𝕾𝖊𝖆

The old man sat there. He must compose himself. He dare not look at Mrs. Bonawitz. She must think him a madman, a fool, or both. He felt rather than saw her take the tray, heard her shoes on the stairs, then snatches of what she related caustically to her man in the kitchen.

The guttural of their distant voices troubled him again, rising and falling, reminding him of the hidden enemy. Who was this undisclosed foeman whose heavy tones had the power to chill his blood, to suck light and color from the day? The boy had given no clue to his identity, had refused to answer, and yet it was obvious that he knew him. The one they both feared and hated was not far from here.

Through the walls for a moment he heard his father's voice, impatient, tinged with gloom. No, it couldn't be he, John Donner told himself. Why, no man was liked more warmly over town and countryside including Broad Mountain. His jovial hackneyed sayings that the sons groaned over were hailed in other households, welcome everywhere.

"Good night, don't let the bedbugs bite," he'd call after young and less young folks on their way to bed. "I'll see you in the morning, in the morning by the bright light, when Gabriel blows his trumpet in the morning." How often had John Donner heard that! No guest was more welcome at another's table or strove harder to earn his keep. His father would sit pleased as Punch at his place, his napkin tucked into his collar, his plate attacked with gusto, his praise for food and hostess without stint or sparing. He had a well-used phrase for every occasion. Let his hostess ask if he wanted water, and he would answer heartily, "Water for me, bright water for me and wine for the trembling debauchee," and when she had put down the glass in front of him, "Your kindness is only exceeded by your good looks." When he could eat no more he would decline with a beaming "I've had an elegant sufficiency, any more would be a superabundance." Aunt Jess, as well as Matt and Polly, thought "the world and all" of him.

And yet John Donner remembered his father a different man at home. As a boy he had never given it much thought.

After all, there was little need for company manners among your family in your own house. He could see his father in his mind now, a dogged figure sitting at the head of the kitchen table, speaking little, insulated, stern, preoccupied with heavy thoughts. Once or twice he had insisted they had forgotten to say grace.

"We didn't pray!" he rebuked them after they had started to eat.

"We did!" the family protested but he silenced them with a look seldom seen on fathers today, the glance of authority and reproach that said, "Do you mean I pray and don't know it, like the heathen?" Propping his right arm again on the table, he lowered his forehead to his hand and waited for them to lay down forks and spoons and dutifully hear him go through the familiar phrases once more. As a guest in another's house his prayer was elaborate as befitted a Sunday-school superintendent aspiring to the ministry, filled with Biblical phrases, "handy with preacher talk," as Annie used to say of him, the supplication closing with the words, "Bless these bounties prepared by kind hands, feed us with the bread of Heaven and at last save us. We ask it in His name, Amen." At home there must have been no special bounties or need, for the end was shortened simply to "Bless this food and us to thy service, Amen."

There was a difference also in his father's singing at home and abroad. Standing by the piano at Aunt Jess's or in some other house, his favorite, "Tired, Oh, Yes, So Tired, *Dear*," was just a musical performance, a "rendition" as it was politely called in Guild circles.

> *Tired, oh, yes, so tired, dear.*
> *The day has been so long.*
> *Sweet smiling faces thronged my side*
> *When the early sunshine shone.*
> *But they grew tired long ago*
> *And they softly sank to rest*
> *With folded hands and brow of snow*
> *On the cold Earth Mother's breast.*

At home the same words by the same singer poured out feelingly to his own ears seemed a personal confession, a weariness with life, bringing the odor of grave clothes into the house.

There was another of his father's favorites that troubled the boy:

Near, near thee, my son,
Stands the old wayside cross,
Like a gray friar cowled
In lichens and moss.

The rest of the family paid it scant attention. It was just the Lichens and Moss Song. But to the child, John Donner, there was something else. *Lear*, a play he read with more liking as a boy than a man, didn't have it. But when in later years he read Sophocles he recognized a fellow doomsman in Oedipus. Oedipus would understand how he felt, the omen of the unfavorable words, the foreboding chorus, the fateful way his father drew it all out, the inescapable doom that lay close ahead, the dread of which would evaporate only in the sunlight of tomorrow morning.

Tomorrow morning was a long way off tonight. Already shadows were taking over the room.

"Mrs. Bonawitz? Could I have a light?" he called.

There was no answer and he called again. Where in God's name was that woman? As a younger man he would have leaped up and got a light for himself. But as a younger man the dark wouldn't have bothered him. Why was it that baseless anxiety attacked age and childhood, least able to fend for themselves? It was one of the miscalculations of creation, or was it? Could there be any trouble next door, he wondered. Might Mrs. Bonawitz have been called to his mother? He remembered as a boy seeing her there during the mysterious attacks his mother had suffered much of her life. As the oldest son he had more than once sent Gene for the doctor and then sat with her, letting her grip his hands against the pain. When he held her wrists he noticed her pulse very fast. Every few beats it fell like a wounded doe. The doctor had called the attacks acute indigestion. John Donner guessed they would be heart attacks today, perhaps something else tomorrow.

"What's the matter?" he shouted bitterly. "Why doesn't somebody answer me?"

After a moment he heard a harsh voice repeating the impatient words in his ear. He listened and his flesh crept. It was the voice he had feared since childhood, had sought and never found, heavy, ominous, dragging up with it intimations of terror from the deep. Now, how had the voice of the frightener come into this room? Surely it was not his own that he heard, still hanging in the air? Why, they always said he had a voice like his father's, a rich singing voice, a lot of vibrant timbre in it, a speaking voice that "carried over 'long distance.' "

He struggled to sit up in bed. Through the gloom he could see a face staring back at him through the mirror of the oaken bureau. Could such be himself, this monster, the hair cruelly thin, the skull revealed, the coarsened smear of a face, the confusion of features once so indubitably his own, now run together as if returning to primordial chaos, the thickened shapelessness of cheeks and jaws, he who had been such a slim youth? At the same time he thought he could see staring back at him from the face most of those ancient kinfolk he had known as a boy, in person or hanging in heavy frames on the wall, the thick short neck of his choleric Grandfather Donner, the trap of a mouth of his Great-Grandmother Stricker, his Great-Uncle Timothy's arrogant nose, the bitter look in the eyes of his Grandmother Morgan who had to die before she had her children raised, and all the other grim, forbidding features of ancestors he couldn't name but who had looked aged at forty. He had thought them long since dead, buried, disintegrated. Instead they had lived on, endured. They were the real survivors. So long as his flesh had flourished, his vitality had kept them down. Now that it had waned, they had come up out of him like a den of turtles swarming over a rock.

He remembered again how the boy had looked at him when asked the identity of the frightener. So that was why he wouldn't reply! It was the great deception practiced by man on himself and his fellows, the legend of hate against the father so the son need not face the real and ultimate abomination, might conceal the actual nature of the monster who haunted the shadows of childhood, whose name only the soul knew and who never revealed himself before the end when it was found that all those disturbing things seen and felt in the father, which as a boy had given him an uncomprehending sense of dread and hostility, were only intimations of his older self to come, a self marked with the inescapable dissolution and decay of his youth. Even the creator of the hate-against-the-father legend must in his bitter later years have guessed the truth.

There were heavy steps on the stairs. Light rose and fell, spreading into the room.

"What's going on in here?" Mr. Bonawitz demanded, lamp in hand.

"It was getting a little dark," the old man stammered.

"Dark, is it?" Mr. Bonawitz said. He was Pennsylvania

Dutch but, like most hard-coal miners, spoke with the Welsh-Irish brogue of the Patch. "You ever work inside? Well, then you don't know what dark is. I don't care how black it gets up here at night, you can always see a little. Even in the house. Under the ground it's different. It's dark already going down the slope. The mountain closes over you and when you get to the eighth level you're half a mile down. If your lamp goes out and you're working somewheres alone, you're lost. You might as well have no eyes. The water drips over you and the rats are waiting to feed on you. You can't see either one. Everything's black. You get to thinking there's no such thing as light left in the world. It's all gone out."

He set the lamp on the bureau, turned it down economically and went on talking about underground workings and abandoned black shafts where the sound of falling water told of abysses far below from which, once fallen into, the victim could never hope to rise.

When the miner left, the man in bed was conscious only of the precious light, of the tiny yellow flame rising from its brass burner pouring its mysterious substance silently, effortlessly, into every corner. How often when he was sick in bed as a child, this small lamp, or one like it, had been his company and companion. When he partly closed his lids, the light was a star with more points than he could count. If he shut the lids still farther, the points stretched in brilliant golden threads across the room, touching the walls, reaching floor and ceiling, mystical paths brighter than the lamp itself. Opening his eyes wide would bring it back again, but he liked it better with lamp bowl and globe fringed with golden fire as the twigs of a bush are ringed with the sun after a rain.

The only time the light failed him was once a fortnight when his mother went "to Guild."

"Good-by. We'll be home long before midnight," she would tell him gaily.

He knew it would be so. And yet despair seized him even before they left, his father to the store, from where, when it closed, he would call at Guild in time for refreshments and to bring his wife home. Until then the small boy would lie sleepless. He never knew why. Like so many other inexplicable and irrevocable things, it just existed. He knew he wasn't alone. His brothers were there and Annie downstairs. But the house was a tomb all the same. The number of minutes in an hour, of hours in an evening, appalled him.

Once eleven o'clock struck, hope in him would start to

rise. He would lie listening for the first footfall in the late street. Mrs. Feezer, a little gray woman like a pouter pigeon, always left Guild early, his mother said. He knew her by her very fast steps, pat, pat, pat, down the dark bricks. Now there was silence again. What he waited to hear was his father bidding good night to the Whetstones. His voice a square away was unmistakable, even on winter nights with the window tightly closed, but the child would not let himself wholly believe or rejoice until the front door opened and he heard the other, the indispensable, voice downstairs.

Then relaxation like a powerful drug bringing with it delectable peace would come over him. It had happened. His mother was home. It was as if she had never been away. In a few minutes her feet would be on the stairs. Shortly she would pass by the door to his bedroom, turning her face to see if he was all right. But almost never did he see her. Even before he heard her hands making pleasant sounds of early readiness for tomorrow's breakfast he was asleep, and only in the morning would he remember how he had tried to stay awake to see her and hear her special good night in their own secret code. She never thought it strange or queer that when he called, "Good night, Mamma," he wanted her to answer, "Good night, Johnny," saying his name with her lips, understanding what he didn't have to explain to her, that to answer merely "good night" after he had said "Good night, Mamma" would have left their nightly farewell dismembered, unfinished, like a sweet tune broken off in the middle and left to dangle all night in the air.

The old man lay very quiet after that. It must be her near presence just across the wall, he thought, that brought back the vanished reality. Using the jar that Mrs. Bonawitz had provided, letting the warm liquid pass, he could feel himself as a boy getting up from bed to make his water at night, sleepy, lazy, conscious of family warmth and security about him and the pleasant things that lay ahead on the morrow. He could see in his mind's eye the wallpaper, not of this room, but of the room across the wall, the green bullrushes and white water with pond-lily leaves flat on it and a yellow and green frog on every third leaf. How often lying abed had he lived in that wallpaper water, swum in it, hid in the rushes and sunned himself with the frog on the floating leaf.

Now lying abed again he was dimly conscious of something unseen coming and trying to push the door wider and hold it open so that more of a boy's world could come in. He

scarcely breathed, fearing to lose it and the unutterable
sensations that drifted over him like soft enveloping clouds.
Those delectable perceptions, how empty of late, how incredibly rich then. He could bring back the certain relish of
box scores in his father's Philadelphia paper, almost to the
tasting of ink and wood pulp; the mouth-watering produced
by words like candy, gum and ice cream; the savory region
of cupboard shelves with the excitement of cinnamon bark
and ginger among which eye and nostrils hunted as if for
gold. Merely the sight of empty plates set on a fresh table
would summon deliciousness, while the sounds and movements
of his mother at the kitchen stove around mealtime fanned in
him delirious expectation.

He changed his position in bed painfully. What was the
secret of a boy's transport getting awake in the morning?
Could pure joy flow from the simple prospect of shedding
confinement in a stuffy house for the endless bright world
outside? From the moment of waking, small bursts of light
in his brain intoxicated, the sounds of a bird or horse, the
glimpse of blue sky through a window, the ample secure
look of his mother's apron at breakfast, the snatched rec-
ollection of peaches or chestnuts hanging on certain trees he

knew, created for him out of nothing, ripened by sun and season, all without cost, to be had for the taking.

What astounded him was that he had once taken this whole world of youth and its possessions as natural, common, all these exquisite impressions running along nerve and blood stream. They were ordinary, to be expected and would never cease. That wonderful youth's staff that came up in him so effortlessly to carry him over bogs and mountains was his own personal nature and property. He had been endowed with it and it would last forever. He questioned it no more than the sun and summer, the freshness of his tissues, his easy conviction that it is, it can, it will be.

The old man lay scarcely moving, observing the boy in him as a living bird within the shell, marvelling at its sure instinct never to observe itself directly, openly, never to examine, analyze or appraise. When he did that, the joy of being died. When he gave mysterious unseen life the rein again, eyes not shrewd or exacting, but dreamy, receptive to the unseen presence and the way that had been provided, letting the chosen things come instead of choosing and going to them, then the magic reality returned. The sun lying where it shone, the bird flying where it flew, the clouds drifting where they drifted, a thousand green leaves bathing him, all joined in the paean. This was the wisdom of age-old youth and which man lost, never to admit the enemy of life, the adult conceit that pleasure or joy could be created or even improved by man's cleverness, by taking it apart, measuring it, weighing, judging and comparing it, even thinking about it, only to bar the soul from consummation of all the prepared wonder and delight.

It was very early when he awoke. A figure stood by his bed. It was Mrs. Bonawitz.

"You get under!" she scolded him, pulling up the covers. "Ai yai, yai. You're sopping wet. That's all Dawdy used to do, sweat, sweat, sweat."

"Do you know the time, Mrs. Bonawitz?" he asked.

"I know it's after four. My man just got off to the early miners' train. And I know you're a Donner. I've been doing the Donners' wash now for six years. I can tell Harry Donner's shirts anyplace once he's wore them. His handkerchiefs, too. His clothes don't smell like other men's clothes. You got the same smell."

So she had noticed his father's scent, that peculiar distillation that as a small boy he fancied all men had, a faint tinge of tobacco but more manly, like the resin of some unknown foreign great-girthed tree. He knew his father used nothing but bay rum, something the son never touched, yet Mrs. Bonawitz said that the mysterious scent marked him, too.

A strong feeling came over him, something like the time as a boy in White Rose Valley he had run four miles home against Gene. By the time they reached the gate his lungs were torn, he could barely move his legs, and he had finished a few feet behind. Just the same when he sank down to the side porch he had felt a clean sense of relief. He didn't have to run any more. He didn't have to prove now that as the oldest he was always the stronger. Also the winner, the stronger, was his brother, of the same blood as he. He was beaten but free.

Now, why should the knowledge that he was after all his father's son give him a corresponding relief and freedom? Was it his earlier discovery that the son-father-hate legend was fiction, after which it had no more power over him; that he and not his father was the monster; and that with all the dissolution and mortality he saw in himself in the glass, he was still the real and true son of his powerful, ever-living father, the participant of his parent's blood and patrimony?

Whether that was it or not, he didn't actually know, only that he felt peace. He listened. The sound of Kronos's rising waters had for the moment ceased. He was home or almost home, very close to his own. This was where he had come into the circumambient layer, where as a tireless young animal he had first inhaled the Vale of Union air. Only a wall, the thinnest of walls, separated him from the bosom of his family.

A rooster crowed and he felt the old boyish joy in the promise of night's end. He heard the steady beat of miners' hobnailed boots tramping up the middle of the street. As a boy the sound had troubled him and his dreams. He didn't know why except it could be the marching, marching, marching, to nothing but blackness underground. Today the rhythmic sound brought back only the pleasant memory of Miss Jones, a summer guest of the Wilberts, who of an afternoon used to sit on the Wilbert porch watching the black-faced men with tin kettles and buckets over their shoulders striding from the miners' train.

"I love to see the colliers come home," she would say in her clipped brogue. "It takes me back to my childhood in Wales."

He lay in ease, quietly remembering. "Oh, I'm so comfortable," he would say to Mrs. Bonawitz when she brought his breakfast. He could hear her coming now and with her step the sound of padding and nail-clicking on the stairs. Then she came with the yellow tray and behind her, his bushy tail slowly waving with each step, was Sandy, the old-time shepherd dog on the snapshot in his pocket.

"He belongs to the Donners," she said. "He comes over every morning for something to eat."

Before he reached the bed, the big dog stopped. The hair on the back of his neck rose and he growled menacingly. Almost at once they heard a rapping on the front door. Mrs. Bonawitz left, the dog galloping ungainly after. John Donner wasn't aware when the woman returned. He looked up and saw her there and knew instantly something had happened. There was a look in her face and eyes that women have when their knowledge exceeds yours.

"It was somebody for you," she said.

"My mother?" he asked eagerly.

"It was a man."

"But nobody knows I'm here except Mr. Bonawitz and the doctor," he protested.

"You said your name was John Donner. Well, that's who he said he wanted, the old man, not the boy."

The first finger of apprehension touched him.

"Did he say what he wanted?"

"He told me he's come to take you home."

Something in those simple words terrified him.

"Did you tell him I can't walk?"

"He says you don't need to. Don't you have a machine you came here with? Well, it brought you here and it'll carry you off, he claims, without your having to do a thing."

The old man got himself under control.

"Was he light or dark?"

"He was dark," she said.

"Did he give his name?"

"He said you wouldn't know his name but he has 'Guard' printed on his cap."

John Donner lay there trying to meet it, to think it through. Somewhere within himself he felt a great yielding, as if the sum and substance of countless hopes, strivings, struggles, answers and resolves had suddenly subsided and grown still. He could go now, if he had to. He had found a part of what he sought. He had learned the identity of the frightener, that it was not his father. He saw the father a little clearer now and that he was his son. As for the rest that he and other men hunted all their lives, was he never to find it? Was it part of the great mystery, of yesterday and to-morrow, of night and the day star, of the nameless and un-spoken? Would he never stand again in the room of the photograph with the light streaming under the closed door? For forty years he had wanted to open that door and see for himself what lay beyond.

Through the wall he heard the strong living strokes of his father's hammer nailing up some box or barrel intended for the new house in River Grove now denied him. The sound brought back another song of his father's.

> *I'm a pilgrim*
> *And I'm a stranger.*
> *I can tarry, I can tarry*
> *But a night.*

Its words to him had always been mystical and obscure, like the communion hymns in church when men and women moved like sad prisoners up the aisle. When he was very young and his father's voice came to the lines "Do not detain me, for I am going, to where the streamlets of life are flow-ing. I'm a pilgrim, and I'm a stranger. I can tarry, I can tarry but a night," it had been as if there were hidden reservations in his father's relations to them, secret commitments he was hinting at, that he only "tarried" with them for tonight, wasn't really someone they knew but a "stranger" whom they could detain no longer, and tomorrow he would vanish from whence he had come, leaving neither trace nor support but only a void and the great enigma.

Today the mysticism and secrecy had lifted from the words and it seemed the simplest and veriest truth his father had sung. Lying there he was aware of a clarity in something else that had been incomprehensible before. When he was a young man leaving home for his first job, his father had embarrassed him.

"Before you go, let us pray," he had said. The young man had had to kneel down with the rest of the family and hear his father go through the long painful formula. He remembered some of the words.

"Bless the member of this household setting forth from our midst to earn his bread by the sweat of his brow. Be with him and let thy face shine upon him and be gracious unto him while we are absent one from the other." The son's name was never mentioned but it had abashed him all the same.

Each time he came home on a visit he had to go through the ordeal again before "setting forth." He had thought it sanctimonious, unnecessary, that it shamed his young dignity and sensibilities.

But strangely in memory today, its pious flavor had fled, leaving a ribbed testament of family bonds, an undeclared but indubitable declaration of belonging, a circle of security, protection and love. He had once thought it empty practice. Now he could feel substance in those distant prayers and kneelings. He had thought the transaction born of the church, of the gloom his father carried with him, a dark cloud brought into the room at parting to chill and frighten. Now he could see that the cloud came from elsewhere, from uncontrollable sources, that his father had fought that cloud all his life with what forces at his command, and they were more powerful forces than the boy had realized, born of the strong fiber and convictions of his time.

He believed that his father would come and kneel down by his bed if he asked for him. But to be prayed for as an old stranger would not be the same. His mother's presence would be something else. Her prayers were tender, personal, like the songs she sang, "There were three ships come sailing in," and "I've a letter from thy sire, baby mine." He couldn't be a stranger to her. Something in her intimate being would know. She need only come into the room and invisible currents would light up between them. He could scarcely wait. She had promised yesterday that he would see her "tomorrow" and she had never told him a falsehood yet.

A NOTE ON THE AUTHOR

Conrad Richter was born in Pennsylvania, the son, grandson, nephew, and great-nephew of clergymen. He was intended for the ministry, but at thirteen he declined a scholarship and left preparatory school for high school, from which he was graduated at fifteen. After graduation he went to work. His family on his mother's side was identified with the early American scene, and from boyhood on he was saturated with tales and the color of Eastern pioneer days. In 1928 he and his small family moved to New Mexico, where his heart and mind were soon captured by the Southwest. From this time on he devoted himself to fiction. *The Sea of Grass* and *The Trees* were awarded the gold medal of the Societies of Libraries of New York University in 1942. *The Town* received the Pulitzer Prize in 1951.

A NOTE ON THE TYPE

This book is set in a type called Scotch. Even though there is a divergence of opinion regarding its exact origin, a cutting of such a face was undertaken and recorded by Messrs. Miller & Richard, of Edinburgh, in 1808. Their specimen sheet of 1812 shows the undeniable features of the face. It is the "Scotch" version of a general renewal of style, the change-over from the pen-derived "Old Style" to the tectonically conceived "Modern" caused by the Didot-Bodoni revolution of the late eighteenth century. Its essential characteristics are sturdy capitals, full rounded lower-case letters, the graceful fillet of the serifs, and a general effect of crispness through sharply contrasting thicks and thins. Composed, printed, and bound by Kingsport Press, Inc., Kingsport, Tennessee. Paper manufactured by S. D. Warren Company, Boston. Typography and binding design by George Salter.

DATE DUE

PRINTED IN U.S.A.